THE BAMBOO BEARS

The Life and
Troubled Times
of the
Giant Panda

Clive Roots

HYPERION PRESS

1989

Hyperion Press Limited gratefully acknowledges the
continued support of Canada Council and the Manitoba
Arts Council.

ISBN 0-920534-61-9

Design by Leo R. Simoens
Typography by Raeber Graphics Inc.
Color separations by GB Graphics Inc.
Printing and binding by Premier Printing Ltd.

PRINTED IN CANADA

Canadian Cataloging in Publication Data

Roots, Clive, 1935-
    The bamboo bears: the life and troubled times of
the giant panda

Bibliography: p.
Includes index.
ISBN: 0-920534-61-9

1. Giant pandas.   I. Title.
QL737.C214R66 1989   599.74'443   C89-098051-9

THE BAMBOO BEARS

For Jean,
who has shared my concern
for animals for many years.
"Poor pandas" she said, while
typing the first draft of this
book.

About the Author

Wally Gloag

Clive Roots has been involved with zoo animals most of his life and since 1970 has been the director of the Assiniboine Park Zoo in Winnipeg, Canada. He is an acknowledged expert in the trapping and acclimatization of wild animals and has collected zoo specimens in South America, the West Indies, and Canada. He is also an international authority on the care and reproduction of softbilled birds, and the care of zoo animals in cold climates. Because of his special interests the Winnipeg zoo now includes over 1250 animals of which several are extinct in the wild and an extensive collection of softbilled birds contained in the zoo's Tropical House.

Clive Roots is Canada's most experienced zoo design, development, and management professional and he has been extensively involved in the design and operation of landscaped and tropically planted zoo displays. Besides guiding Winnipeg's zoo activities he is active as a zoological consultant to many major Canadian zoos and wildlife associations and has been invited to present papers at conferences throughout the world. His bird expertise is well known and he has achieved first world breedings of many species including the little bee-eater, the yellow oriole, and the blue whistling thrush.

Clive Roots is interested in conservation and over the years has contributed extensively to the dissemination of knowledge and information on the protection of endangered animals and the preservation of their habitats in numerous articles, scientific papers, radio and TV shows, and lectures. He is the author of many books and has provided entries for the *International Encyclopedia of Pets,* the *World Encyclopedia of Birds,* and *Encyclopedia Canadiana.* As a founder-member and chairman of the steering committee he was actively involved in the formation of the Canadian Association of Zoological Parks and Aquariums. His most recent interest in conservation is with the Giant Panda. The Chinese government offered two pandas to the Assiniboine Park Zoo and the animals will visit Winnipeg for four months in the summer of 1989.

Contents

Credits

Photographs courtesy of the following:
Bill Meng, New York Zoological Society, 10 (bottom), 60, 96
Bruce Coleman, 21
Chapultepec Zoo, Mexico City, 68 (top and bottom left)
Chicago Zoological Society, 28
Chris Junck, Calgary Zoo, 68 (bottom right)
Clive Roots, 15, 40, 43
Craig W. Racicot, Zoological Society of San Diego, 51, 95
D. Demello, New York Zoological Society, x
Field Museum of Natural History, Chicago, 26
Great Circus of China, 91
Image 2, 67
J. Allan Cash Ltd., 81
L. Dominguez, Zoo de Madrid, 34 (top), 65
Los Angeles Zoo, 17
Metropolitan Toronto Zoo, 89
Neal Johnston, Los Angeles Zoo, 9, 45, 86
New York Zoological Society, 32 (bottom)
R. Frese, West Berlin Zoo, 56
Ron Garrison, Zoological Society of San Diego, ii
WWF/Timm Rautert, Bruce Coleman, 6-7, 12, 22-23, 76, 79
Zoological Society of London, 10 (top), 32 (top), 34 (bottom)
Zoological Society of San Diego, front cover, 2, 38, 62, 88, 92, 99

Figures

Poaching and forest
clearance are the major
threats to the panda's
survival.

Introduction

This is the story of an animal that survived for millions of years only to become entangled in less than a century in the inevitable process of extermination. The principles are familiar, but the case is special because it is the giant panda's story. It began long ago when a carnivore became the cuddly bamboo-eating bear that has since enthralled the world. Now its end approaches rapidly, and may be final, as the hazards and controversies of the modern era threaten to overwhelm the panda. Such an ending would be tragic for it is the most special animal of all. China's national treasure and its animal ambassador of goodwill, symbol of the World Wildlife Fund and of international conservation, and one of the most endangered large mammals, the panda is indeed a unique creature. It is the most appealing, the most desirable, and yet the most controversial animal alive. Its appearance, behavior, and rarity, and its remote and mysterious homeland have made it a legend in its lifetime. But the panda's hold on life has become tenuous, for mankind needs its mountainous habitat and desires its furry pelt — no longer as a sleeping rug in a hunter's hut but as a $100,000 status symbol in a Hong Kong or Tokyo penthouse.

The panda's value has been recognized since early this century — dead at first for museums, then alive for zoos. Both coveted the panda, for they were institutions dependent upon visitors for their own survival and the visitors were attracted by the pandas. Soon the demand far exceeded the supply and this only increased the panda's appeal and value. It became the only animal able to attract thousands of extra visitors to a zoo, even to double the normal attendance and stimulate the selling of countless souvenirs and novelties, from T-shirts and pins to puppets and postcards.

Despite the lack of publicity and marketing agents and the benefits of today's promotional campaigns the arrival of pandas in the West fifty years ago created tremendous interest and curiosity. When the very first one, Su-lin, arrived at San Francisco in 1936 there were unprecedented scenes of excitement that rivaled the greatest welcome ever given to a foreign celebrity. Later, crowds flocked to Chicago's Brookfield Zoo to see her. Two years after that New York's Bronx Zoo was overwhelmed with visitors to see another panda, Pandora. Londoners responded similarly to their first live panda, Ming, on her arrival in the winter of 1938. Shrewd zoo officials hid her in a vain attempt to postpone her debut until spring when larger crowds could be expected, but there was such a public outcry that she was immediately put on show for three hours daily. Attendance records fell as thousands of extra visitors came

The panda is the only
animal able to
dramatically increase a
zoo's annual attendance.

to see her, including Queen Mary and the Princesses Royal, Elizabeth and Margaret.

As the years went by pandas became even bigger attractions and the few zoos that received them took advantage of their appeal and charm, and saw their attendances flourish. Chi Chi, who lived in the London Zoo for almost fourteen years, was visited by over twenty-five million people, and seen by many more on television. The chances of acquiring pandas permanently ended in 1982, but soon afterwards China set a new precedent by sending a pair on loan to the Los Angeles Zoo to celebrate the XXI Olympic Games. This gave Western zoos another opportunity. There was an almost embarrassing rush to take advantage of this new way of acquiring pandas, if only on loan for a few months. Hundreds of thousands of extra visitors converged on zoos in the United States, Canada, Ireland, Australia, Japan, and Europe as they received panda "visitors." When international criticism and a lawsuit brought an end to the short-term panda loans there were thirty institutions in the United States alone negotiating for them. No other living wild animal could have achieved such fame and attention. Only the creatures of myth and fantasy — the sasquatch, centaur, or Loch Ness monster — or the real-life but long-dead mammoth, and no doubt the first creature from outer space, could outdraw the panda.

What makes the panda such a fascinating and charming animal? Simply its appearance and behavior. Its large, flat face with big eyes like teardrops, and its dumpy, plushy black and white body are its most important attributes. It appeals to maternal instincts because it looks like a living teddy bear, needing to be cuddled and protected. The panda's ability to sit up and hold objects in its big furry paws, its clumsiness, playfulness, and perceived friendliness to humans adds to its attraction. And baby pandas, those perfect miniatures of their bumbling parents! Their charms are so irresistible that even veteran panda hunters Theodore and Kermit Roosevelt and Dean Sage were immediately converted to panda lovers after playing with Su-lin. They pronounced they could never shoot another panda, unfortunately not a sentiment shared by modern panda poachers.

Prior to Su-lin the panda was a prime target for big game hunters and museum collectors, but as she charmed the West, so the West's attitude to pandas changed. The attitude in China changed also and no more "foreign devils" expeditions were allowed to search Sichuan's mountain slopes to supply museums and zoos. The Chinese government allowed only a few pandas to be exported overseas as official gifts, and began to develop policies for their protection. But these policies produced even more disagreement and controversy.

The panda may be the most appealing animal in the world, but it is also the most controversial, and since its discovery it has been the subject of many disputes. Is it extinct already, they wondered at the turn of the century? Is it a bear or a raccoon? Does it eat only bamboo? Does it climb trees? These questions have since been answered, some after considerable study and debate. But others remain unsolved. For example, who really did acquire Su-lin, the first live panda seen in the West? Did pandas hibernate before they became bamboo-eaters, and does their startling black and white coat camouflage or advertise them? More recently there are other, more important questions, and the panda's survival depends on finding the right answers.

They concern the very policies intended to protect the panda. Conservationists now question the value of short-term loans to Western zoos, believing they are detrimental to the panda's long-term survival. There is also disagreement over whether pandas should be left where they are or removed from the wild for their security and captive breeding — a question asked many times of other endangered species. But captive breeding has so far not been the answer to panda survival. These concerns, and others, have led to the most crucial question of all, "What is the best way to conserve the panda?" The answer to this dilemma would determine if China's handling of the present situation is in the panda's best interests.

The panda has always been rare, but in this century it has become endangered. It was already scarce when news of its existence first reached the West. Its range then was a fraction of its earlier pre-human distribution and it was difficult to find in the bamboo forests. In the past fifty years about two hundred pandas have been shot for museums or caught for zoos, including those in China. The recent bamboo die-offs in the mid 1970s and the early 1980s are believed to have killed about two hundred and fifty pandas, and poaching in recent years has accounted for perhaps another two hundred and fifty. Allowing also for the reduction of its habitat since Pere David first reported its existence little more than a century ago, it is likely that its numbers then were not much greater than double the current population of about a thousand individuals. But once in motion the processes of extinction accelerate and the apex of the panda pyramid is approaching with a momentum that will be difficult, if not impossible, to stop.

Although poaching still endangers the wild pandas, the most serious threat to their survival is the clearing of the mountainside vegetation for farming or bamboo and firewood gathering. The small panda population is fragmented and this will cause insurmountable breeding and genetic problems in the long term. But none of this is of any consequence if the panda cannot survive the short term. And this may happen because it cannot migrate to other areas for food when the bamboo dies. So the future of the bamboo bear depends not only on its protection but also on the preservation of western China's forested mountains.

The panda is the symbol of hope for wild animals and their wild places. No other endangered species, and probably no other wild animal, has ever had such a high profile. Its survival, more than that of any other creature, will prove that conservation can work. But to date it has not, and George Schaller, the West's greatest authority on pandas, has said "no face-saving illusions can hide the fact that efforts to save the species have so far failed." All the millions of dollars, all the scientific expertise, advice, criticism, and public concern may not be able to save the panda. If it becomes the twenty-first century's dodo it will only prove what has been suspected, and perhaps known, for many years. That there really is not a great deal of hope for any large wild animals on this planet.

The Golden Mountains

1

Of all the
creatures that
inhabit China's
Golden Mountains
the giant panda is
the most golden of
them all.

Mountains shrouded in mist and mystery cover the southwestern corner of China, separating the coastal lowlands from the high Tibetan plateaus. Crowding the eastern edge of the Himalayas they were formed of sandstone, limestone, dolomite, and granite long ago, before even dinosaurs roamed the earth. Time and vegetation smoothed them and they became a wilderness area of high peaks and deep valleys, tranquil mountain lakes and dense evergreen forest. They lie at the junction of three of the world's climatic zones — the cold and arid Tibetan highlands, the temperate north, and the tropics of southern China — and each contributed its distinctive climate and plant and animal life to the region.

Although the area is only a few hundred miles north of the tropics, the climate of the mountains is extreme. Mild in the valley bottoms, it is as harsh as the Arctic on the snow-clad peaks. Precipitation is high, for the moisture carried across China from the Pacific Ocean by the southeast monsoon winds condenses when they meet the mountain barrier. Rocky stream beds carry the water back down the valleys to the tributaries of the Yangtze River and then to the ocean. In summer the heavy rainfall creates an atmosphere of almost perpetual dampness, and the highest peaks are wrapped in mist and cloud. Colder temperatures arrive in October, and from then until March snow falls heavily on the mountainsides and is several centimeters deep when the spring thaw begins. Many of the peaks exceed sixty-five hundred meters and have permanent snow caps. Minya Konka, the highest, reaches almost eight thousand meters into the clouds. Like all the mountains outside the polar circles their slopes have definite vegetation zones.

Immediately below the peaks there is a region known as the alpine desert where the climate is too harsh and the rockscape too barren for all but a few small plants. From the lower limit of this rock and snow zone down to the tree line at about four thousand meters there are alpine meadows reminiscent of the Arctic tundra. Snow-covered all winter, these steeply sloping grasslands bloom in spring with a colorful carpet of gentians, primroses, and worts of many kinds — ragworts, fumeworts, and louseworts. The mammalian life of the meadows reflects the same zone in North America's Rockies, but in the Chinese setting the grizzly bear is replaced by its close relative the brown bear, the largest animal there, and also one of the rarest. Small mammals are plentiful, with numerous rodents and insect-eaters such as voles, pikas or mouse hares, shrews of several kinds, and one which is a unique combination of shrew

Previous page
Shrouded in mist and
mystery, China's south-
western mountains are
home to many rare and
endangered animals.

Opposite
The golden monkey is
China's number two
national treasure.

and mole and lives nowhere else. The bears hunt these small mammals, but they are no longer truly carnivorous and eat far more vegetation than meat. The snow leopard is the largest hunter on the alpine heights, lying in ambush and overpowering the fleet-footed bharal or blue sheep after a short chase over the rocks. Birds are scarce. A few hawks circle high over the meadows searching for rodents. Carrion-seeking ravens look for the remnants of a snow leopard's meal and rock buntings, snow pigeons, and the lovely monal pheasant search for seeds and succulent shoots.

Prevented by the harsh winters from edging into these meadows, the permanent glossy green mantle of the rhododendron forest dominates the vegetation zone immediately below the tree line. A narrow band, with a scattering of spruce and fir trees, it descends less than one thousand meters before merging with the bamboo. Although it is ever-green, in comparison with the other zones on the mountainsides there are relatively few animals in this moist dense rhododendron belt. Species from either side of the zone stray into it, or pass through, but it has few residents.

Below the rhododendrons the bamboo forest is the dominant plant zone of the mountains. It is a band two thousand meters wide on most slopes, ending at fifteen hundred meters above sea level. Here the living canes of many species of bamboo are shaded by the more familiar trees of the northern temperate regions. Deciduous maple, poplar, willow, and birch, and evergreen spruce, fir, and hemlock grow alongside rare endemic species like the Chinese dove tree. Vines and low deciduous shrubs grow here also, but the bamboo dominates, to be measured not in hectares but by the square kilometer. Below it the deciduous and coniferous forest extends to the valley bottoms.

These central and lower sections of the mountain slopes form a unique habitat. They are rich in plant life of many shades of green, the type of forest born of a temperate climate and heavy rainfall. But this forest is also a storehouse of other natural treasures, for it harbors some of the rarest and most distinctive animals. It is one of the world's golden regions where the golden pheasant, golden cat, golden monkey, and golden takin live. And the panda, despite its coloring, is the most golden of them all. Its life inextricably entwined with the bamboo, and completely dependent upon it for food, the panda for three million years has survived the bamboo's mysterious eccentricities as it died off over huge areas several times each century.

Bird life on the mid and lower slopes is abundant, with many wagtails, redstarts, jay thrushes, babblers, wrens, and titmice. Some are resident all year; others visit for the summer. It is a stronghold also of the small mammals, not so colorful in their greys and browns, but making them-selves known nevertheless. There are squirrels, shrews, rats, mice, and voles of many kinds, and the bamboo rat, which resembles a large fat mole more than the familiar rat. But as always the larger animals are the most impressive and most noticeable, and the variety living there makes the Southwestern mountains the greatest mammal region in the north-ern hemisphere.

China's other national treasure, the snub-nosed golden monkey, second only to the panda in esteem, lives in the trees above the bamboo groves, where its thick coat of burnished gold protects it from the snow and winter winds. A vegetarian, it eats bamboo as the panda does but also varies this boring diet with other leaves, buds, and berries. Another panda lives there also, a much smaller reddish-brown and white animal known as Styans panda, the local representative of the red panda that lives farther west, high on the southern slopes of the Himalayas. More species of ungulates or hoofed mammals live on these mountainsides than in any other region of northern Eurasia or North America. Deer are the most plentiful species, the northern temperate ones extending south to mingle with the tropical species at the northern end of their distribution. In size they range from the large sambhar and the rare white-lipped deer to the whippet-sized musk deer and tufted deer. Wild boar also roam the hillsides in small bands eating everything edible, digging for roots, chomping grass, gorging on acorns, and scavenging the bones of long-dead animals. They are equally at home on the plains of Sichuan or in the high bamboo forest, and have the widest altitudinal range of all China's hoofed mammals.

The most unusual herbivores in panda country are the takin, serow, and goral, known collectively as the goat antelopes. Zoologically as controversial as the panda, they were believed at first to be antelopes, but are now considered closer relatives of the sheep and goats. The gorals and serows are small cliff-dwellers, but the takin is a much larger animal, weighing up to three hundred and fifty kilograms, and with a Roman

Opposite
The panda does not
hibernate and is active
all winter in the snow.

Below
The panda is no longer
a carnivorous animal. It
eats far more vegetation
than meat.

nose, thick legs, and the horns of a buffalo. Its golden-colored hide may have been Jason's original golden fleece. This diversity of hoofed animals gives the impression of a large resident population of grazers and browsers, but it is a false one for the mountains are rich in variety, not numbers. Most of their animals are loners, and the vegetation cannot support the density of herbivores that live on tropical grasslands, such as East Africa's Serengeti Plains.

Wherever meat-producing animals live, however, those that prey upon them are never far away. With the wealth of small mammals in China's southwestern mountains there is also an abundance of small predators, again many in species not numbers. Weasel, mink, leopard cat, and isabelline lynx live there, together with the red fox, hog badger, and yellow-throated marten. But with the tiger no longer resident, and the panda given to chomping instead of chasing, there are only four large carnivores in the bamboo forests. Two of these are bears, the Himalayan black bear and the Chinese brown bear, which occasionally leaves the alpine heights to raid the mountain's lower levels. Although they are not great hunters they are always eager to seize a newborn deer fawn or a baby panda left hidden in a thicket by its mother.

The other large carnivores are the leopard and the red dog or dhole, which are both hunters. The leopard, a geographical race of the animal that lives in Africa and India, ranges across central and southern China, extending north almost to Beijing. The leopard of Sichuan is brightly colored, with a whitish belly and large black spots and rosettes on a rich orange-red background. It is now one of China's rarest animals, becoming scarcer as its prey dwindles. Like all the large cats except the lion it is a solitary hunter. In contrast the dhole is a relentless pack hunter similar to the northern wolves and the Cape hunting dogs of Africa. It is also the Chinese representative of a species that lives throughout southern and central Asia, including the island of Java. With its rusty-red coat, rounded furry ears, and bushy black-tipped tail it resembles the union of a red fox and a coyote. In cunning, stamina, and agility dholes are the equal of them both and tirelessly follow the trails of deer and wild boar, chasing them to the point of exhaustion before attacking from all sides. None of these predators respects rarity or uniqueness, and the bamboo thickets regularly witness the drama of the hunters seeking their prey, even if that prey is the last surviving white-lipped deer or the most endearing young golden monkey.

The panda evolved in these mountains, high on the slopes alongside so many other unusual animals, each remarkable in its own way, but none so mysterious. It is one of the survivors — vulnerable to the leopard, dhole, and brown bear; able to exist on plants that provide just enough nourishment; and with breeding habits that place its baby at risk throughout its young life. But the panda overcame these difficulties and the golden mountains witnessed one of the most dramatic events of all, that of a carnivore that became a vegetarian and survived in the process. How it did this is one of evolution's most remarkable achievements. But many of the secrets of its success are still locked in the mist shrouding those remote mountains.

Even with its
distinctive black and
white coloring, the
panda is very difficult
to find in the bamboo
groves.

Survival

2

Ambling along the mountain trails, pausing occasionally to chew a bamboo cane or sniff a scent mark, the panda is unmistakable in its furry black and white coat. But its shape is quite unusual. It looks like a small bear, walks like a bear, and when sitting appears to be a rotund, even dumpy animal. Yet when it reaches up against a tree trunk or stretches, yawning, as it leaves its nest den, the panda's body seems too long for its short stubby legs. It is built neither for speed nor for traveling great distances. Addicted to bamboo, and with a regular supply close at hand, it has no need for the large territory of the wide-ranging, omnivorous brown bear, and its home range covers only five square kilometers. It is solitary for most of the year and fraternizes with its own kind only at mating time. Like all loners the panda marks its territorial boundaries to let others know that the area is occupied, using its short, bushy tail to brush scent from its anal glands onto trees and rocks. Good eyesight is obviously not essential for an animal living in thickets of close-packed bamboo, and the panda's vision, like that of the bears, is not acute. Its hearing is well developed, however, and it has a good sense of taste and smell, which seem unnecessary for an animal that eats only bamboo.

Most animals are either active all day or all night, usually in twelve-hour shifts. The panda is different. Since bamboo is a nutritionally poor food, and as the panda needs to keep its stomach full at all times, it alternately eats and sleeps at frequent intervals throughout each twenty-four-hour period. It may eat for fourteen hours on a typical day in summer or winter for it does not hibernate as the other bears in the mountains do. Protected by its thick and rather oily coat from the rain, snow, and cold, and having the furry soles of the polar bear, the panda is out eating bamboo on the coldest winter days. When the snow deepens on the mountainsides the panda's trails become tunnels between the bamboo groves, and other animals, both predator and prey, use them to negotiate the slopes.

Although the panda's daily routine is stereotyped and monotonous, its life is not completely idyllic. The other large carnivores may be uncommon in the mountains and have much larger home ranges as befits more predatory species, but they still appear now and then, and the panda is certainly not safe from them. Both the leopard and the dhole attack pandas when the opportunity arises, although probably just the very old and the very young are the targets. Panda cubs are also vulnerable to black bears, but these are unlikely to bother adult pandas which are

The panda is a solitary animal that spends most of every day, winter and summer, eating bamboo.

The dhole, right, and
the Chinese leopard,
below, are the panda's
major predators.

similar to the bears in size, the males weighing about one hundred and forty kilograms and females a little less. Pandas have another advantage besides size — they have much more powerful jaws. It is the brown bear, however, that is the most serious threat to the panda, for it has the size and strength to overpower all of the mountain's animals, including the other predators. Only habitual tree-dwellers are safe from it.

As hunters, the leopards and dholes are more interested in the deer, goat-antelopes, and wild swine, which all have highly developed sight, hearing, and speed to give them a fair chance against the wiles and stamina of the carnivores. So how does the plodding panda fare against these predators? With its poor eyesight and top speed of little more than a clumsy trot, it could never outrun a leopard or a pack of dholes. Although it can glide almost silently through the packed bamboo stems, they are no protection against the leopard which lies in ambush until its prey is within easy reach or against the dholes which would soon pick up the panda's trail again as it crossed a clearing. The panda's shape and bumbling habits provide the answer, for they result as much from the lack of pressure to escape its enemies by speed as from the lack of need to chase prey. The panda would never have survived to the present day if it was easy game, and it certainly is not without means of protecting itself. In fact the panda is a formidable foe. It has powerful jaws and teeth, heavy forepaws equipped with sharp claws, and tremendous strength in its shoulders. As the black bears do when danger threatens, the panda relies on its tree-climbing skills to give it added protection, especially from the dholes and brown bears that cannot climb.

Animals are usually most vulnerable to predators when they are young, particularly at the beginning of life if they are left unguarded by their parents, and then later when they go off into the world on their own. The panda is no exception and these are the times when predation is heaviest. In addition the panda's strange breeding habits increase the danger to its offspring. Winters are cold and inhospitable in the mountains, but when the low temperatures arrive the babies of most animals that were born the previous spring are independent and can withstand the inclement weather and decreased food supplies. The northern bears are exceptions, for they give birth in the safety of a den and stay there with their cubs until the spring thaw. This is an excellent survival mechanism for small and helpless cubs during the first few months of their lives. Yet the panda developed none of these strategies to safeguard its young. Its reproductive habits are a puzzle, for they almost contradict survival. Even though twin births are common, the panda can only cope with one cub, and the odds appear against it raising even that.

Pandas begin to breed when they are five years old, and seek a mate any time between March and May, yet births usually occur in late summer. Their gestation period has varied from ninety-seven days to one hundred and sixty-three days, but such a wide range of continual development is impossible, therefore delayed egg-implantation must occur. Similar to the black bear's reproduction method, the fertilized panda eggs are probably implanted in the uterus wall and commence their development just two months or so before birth. Giving birth in

late summer the panda must then protect its helpless baby not only from predators but also from the weather through the worst time of the year.

As the time of birth approaches, the pregnant panda finds a suitable den site, usually a hollow in the base of a large tree or in a wide rock crevice, where she builds a nest of branches. The newborn cubs resemble those of the other bears in size and in the state of their development. They weigh just one hundred and twenty-five grams and are only sixteen centimeters long and are therefore almost a thousand times smaller than their mothers. They are blind, helpless, and toothless, and are covered with sparse white hair through which their pink skin shows. Their distinctive markings begin to appear when they are a week old, when a black fuzz grows around their eyes and on their ears and

Opposite
Baby pandas are most
vulnerable to predation
when they are left
alone in the dens while
the mothers go out to
feed.

shoulders, and a few days later over their limbs. Initially their eye patches are circular but by the end of their first month the patches are oblong "teardrops" like the mother's. The panda's cubbing den is open to the elements, not sealed and heated by her body as in a hibernating bear's den. As the days, and especially the nights, begin to cool, baby pandas are cradled in their mothers' paws to keep them warm and protected, and are cuddled to her chest when they need to suckle. But this tender care can be given to only one cub, and even though the panda usually gives birth to twins and occasionally to triplets, only one survives to face the other hazards.

When raising her cub the mother panda receives no help from its father. There is no bond between them, and she probably has not even seen him since the spring mating. She must search for her own regular supplies of bamboo even when she is lactating, and although her food supplies are close at hand the baby is left unattended when she goes off to eat. This is the most vulnerable period of its life, for the small, defenseless cub is at the mercy of all the mountain's predators, down to the size of the weasel.

By the time the panda cub is one month old it is fully furred, and it then accompanies its mother on her foraging trips. She clutches it to her chest when she travels and caches it nearby when she stops to eat. It is mid-October by then and winter has set it on the higher slopes. The other bears are no longer a threat because they have already entered hibernation. They will not menace the panda cub again until they reappear from their dens the following spring — a time when an active young panda may be separated from its mother. By then the baby panda will be eight months old, will weigh about thirteen kilograms, and although no longer dependent upon its mother's milk, will continue to benefit from her guidance and protection for another year until she seeks a mate again. At that stage of its life, similar to black bear cubs, it can climb trees to escape the brown bears and dholes, but it is still vulnerable to a number of tree-climbing predators such as the yellow-throated marten, lynx, and leopard.

Despite all these hazards there is surprisingly little natural predation of wild pandas. Perhaps this is because of the relative scarcity of large predators and the relative abundance of the true herbivores, which are their favored prey. Although it may seem far easier and more productive for them to tackle the sedentary panda than to lie in ambush for hours or chase ruminants and swine up and down the mountains before making a kill, these efforts in terms of the return, and the ease of overcoming the prey without a serious fight, are obviously more worthwhile. Does the panda's coloring offer another reason why it has survived? Does the black and white coat provide protection from predators, helping it to blend with the snow and shadows in winter and with areas of bright sunlight and shade in summer? Probably not. It seems to be no safer than its relatives, the black and brown bears, that are uniformly dark in color, although the race of the brown bear in China is a lighter shade than most. Their greater size likely protects the other bears from leopards and dholes, but they fall prey to wolves and the Siberian tiger farther north.

If, however, the panda's coloring is good camouflage, who is it hiding from? The leopard hunts mainly by sight and is attracted by the movement of its prey, and the dholes track by scent. If these animals did track the panda, is it likely that after a lengthy ambush or a long, exciting chase the leopard or the dhole would back off when close enough to their prey to see that it was black and white? Which raises another interesting possibility. Is the reverse true? Could the panda be boldly marked to advertise its presence, rather than conceal it, as the skunk warns predators of its spraying potential? Perhaps the panda's coloring does warn predators. For an inoffensive vegetarian its bamboo-crunching jaws are a force to be reckoned with. Yet the black and brown bears of eastern Asia are just as formidable opponents and they are not clad in warning colors. Nor is the spotted hyena of Africa, which has far stronger bone-crushing jaws. The difference lies in the fact that the hyena is a predator and does not need to send out warnings of its presence. Also it is completely nocturnal. Its dull, uniform coloring is obviously an advantage at night. But the skunk is nocturnal too, yet its black and white coloring does not prevent owls and other nighttime predators from attacking it.

The panda's coloring was likely a compromise of several needs, and in spite of it or because of it the panda has coped with all the hazards it has had to face. In its present form it has survived all the natural pressures for a long time. These pressures could not have been overwhelming or a black and white, bamboo-munching, predator-turned-vegetarian could not have evolved on the wet and slippery mountain slopes. Bamboo failures, earthquakes, cold winters, poor quality food, vulnerable babies, distinctive markings, and predators — none of these were enough to overcome the panda's staunch resilience. It is a survivor and it needed to make few changes to its habits or appearance to endure for the last three million years.

Today, however, the very qualities that enabled it to persist are working against it. Can it adapt to its new threats? It seems doubtful, for if it did not change in all those years it cannot change in a century. Yet change it must, for the panda and China's other animal treasures are no longer secure in their former stronghold and their survival cannot be guaranteed for the next century. In addition to the natural hazards which they evolved to combat, they must now cope with the most unrelenting plunderer of all. As so many animals have discovered, this new menace wants their homeland as well.

Discovery

3

Man must have been aware of the panda for a very long time. In his most recent upright forms as *Homo erectus*, archaic man, and then modern man, he has lived in panda country for well over half a million years. From the Lantian archaeological site in central China just west of the panda's remaining habitat there is evidence that the first erect human lived in the region about seven hundred thousand years ago. Records of modern man — about sixty thousand years old from sites such as Ordos and Liujiang in central and southern China plus earlier ones of his less human-like ancestors — indicate the likelihood of an unbroken line of human occupation from the arrival of Lantian man to the present day.

Were these early people acquainted with the panda? It is reasonable to assume that they were. Evolving man's dependency upon wild animals for food and his capacity as hunter must have acquainted him with all the wild animals in his area. Was man a panda hunter? If he was it has yet to be proved. The discovery of panda bones at the campsites or in the hearths of these ancient people may eventually shed light on this, but right now there is no evidence that early Chinese man hunted the panda. And the obvious question is, "Why would he need to?" The panda was not the same kind of threat that the cave bear, cave lion, and sabre-tooth were to other early cultures. Pandas could not provide meat of the quantity and quality of the large grazing or browsing mammals, some of which still live in the mountains and were well within the hunting capacity of early man. Man had proved his capability elsewhere in the northern hemisphere, where his fearless and successful hunting of the megafauna helped to exterminate it after the retreat of the last ice cap about twelve thousand years ago. The only possible value of the panda to early man was as a provider of skins for robes or bedding. But from the time he colonized far-eastern Asia until quite recently, there is no evidence of man's connection with the panda. Man's knowledge of the panda obviously existed, but the association must remain speculative until the bones can prove it.

The discovery and dating of fossils prove that the panda's range in the eighteenth century covered most of the western half of China. Apart from some areas of flat land such as Sichuan's central plain, it is the most mountainous region in the whole country. As the burgeoning population of lowland eastern China pushed farther west, the panda's habitat and numbers shrank as it was forced into the most remote mountain areas

The existence of the black and white bear was first recorded in Pere David's diaries in 1869.

Opposite
The panda's habit of
climbing trees to escape
predators made it
vulnerable to hunters
with guns.

which were bisected by tributaries of the great Chiang Jiang or Yangtze River and populated by aboriginal tribesmen. The remote location combined with its secretive nature made the panda difficult to find even in the twentieth century. These factors isolated it from cultured China until quite recently.

The earliest surviving documents that mention the panda date from 1000 BC, but its name did not occur with any frequency until far more recently. During the western Han Dynasty about two thousand years ago, a panda is said to have been kept alive in the emperor's palace in Xian, and the skull of a panda was apparently buried with the mother of the Dynasty's fourth emperor. In the year 621 AD the first emperor of the Tang Dynasty is recorded to have given fourteen skins of the beishung, the white bear (as the panda seems to have been called), to his subjects. Later in the same Dynasty there is a record of two live white bears sent in 685 AD to the Emperor of Japan, plus seventy skins. If these really were pandas it is difficult to know why they were called white bears when they have so much black on them and the white yellows with age and use.

There has been some speculation that perhaps these early references were of polar bears. Yet their range is the Arctic Circle and does not include China and it would be very unusual for them to stray so far south along the Siberian coast. Also, polar bears would have been more difficult to obtain, for their size and aggressiveness have always made them dangerous adversaries. Even if there was trade between the ancient Chinese and the Siberian natives of the far North, it seems unlikely that seventy polar bear skins could have been accumulated to trade with China, just to be given away. It is just as unlikely that seventy panda skins would have been available as tribute, considering the animal's scarcity, secrecy, and remote habitat. Another explanation has been suggested. These white bears were perhaps brown bears, relatives of the grizzly bears which in China are pale, almost cream-colored animals. But they were no more plentiful in western China than the panda was. The identity of the white bears remains a mystery.

Since the panda has lived side by side with modern man for so many years it is surprising it was not mentioned more often. This did have one advantage, for despite being such a mystic animal the panda's body was never used in traditional medicines. As interest in using animal artifacts developed in China, the panda, even though it was considered a symbol of bravery, was fortunately excluded because so little was known about it in the more civilized eastern parts of the country. For the same reason it did not become prominent in art or legends, as the crane has become. So the panda was virtually an enigma in its own country almost up to the time it became known to the West, less than one hundred and fifty years ago. Catholic missionaries were established in China's interior before then, and Shanghai was already a prosperous international port visited by the vessels of many nations. But it was not until military pressure began to open up China to Westerners that there was any great penetration of the country's interior or investigation of its unique natural history.

Fortunately for Chinese biology one of the first to enter the interior

Previous page Typical
panda habitat. The
dense vegetation and
heavy mist made it very
difficult for the first
Western hunters to
locate pandas.

and record its plants and animals was Abbe Armand David. Born in the Basse-Pyrenees, David became a priest of the Order of St. Vincent de Paul who were known as Lazarists. He joined the Order because he wanted to become a missionary in China. Also interested in wildlife, he sailed for Shanghai in 1862 with commissions from the Paris Museum of Natural History to collect biological material. He sent hundreds of specimens and records back to France, and the Museum's director was so impressed that he arranged for Pere David to be sponsored by the French government for more detailed studies. During the next ten years he made three lengthy journeys into the interior where he suffered severe hardships, several illnesses, and was attacked by bandits. His travels and animal and plant collections made Pere David the most famous naturalist-explorer of his day, and one of the most celebrated of all time. He discovered almost two hundred species of animals and many plants that were new to science in the West. Many were named after him — the most familiar being Pere David's deer or milou, already extinct in the wild when he saw it at the Emperor's palace, and the least familiar a small bird called David's titmouse. He discovered the panda, China's number one wildlife treasure and now by far its most familiar animal, and its second most precious living treasure, the snub-nosed golden monkey, although neither of these animals bears his name.

The reports of other missionaries who had visited China's western mountains and spoken of their strange plants and animals encouraged Pere David to explore that region on his second journey into the interior, which began in the summer of 1868 and lasted two years. Starting at Shanghai he traveled up the Yangtze River to Chongking, a journey that took six weeks in those days. From there he went to Chengdu, and then on to Moupin — to the monastery established earlier in the century where he planned to spend a whole year. His diaries, which were later published in almost unabridged form, first mention the panda on the 11th of March 1869. He was visiting the home of a hunter named Li and wrote in his diary "at this pagan's I see a fine skin of the famous black and white bear which appears very large. It is a very remarkable species and I rejoice when I hear my hunters say that I shall certainly obtain the animal within a short time. They tell me that they will go out as early as tomorrow to kill this carnivore." It is not known why he referred to it as "famous." The hunters did go out the next day and returned ten days later "with a young white bear which they took alive, but unfortunately killed it so it could be carried more easily."

Pere David believed this black and white animal must be a new species of bear, "which was remarkable not only for its color but also for its paws which are hairy underneath." A few days later his hunters brought him another dead panda, an adult this time, whose "colours are exactly the same as the young one I have already, but the black is less pure and the white more soiled." He was more convinced than ever that it was a bear and called it *Ursus melanoleucus,* the black and white bear. He later reported that the new bear was much rarer than the Himalayan black bear in western China and that it was a vegetarian that ate flesh when it could. He assumed that it must be carnivorous in winter. As he never did see a panda in the wild or have an opportunity to study its habits, he relied on information gathered from the hunters.

Pere David's accounts, the skins he sent back to France, and the scientific deliberations they generated at the Paris Museum stimulated great interest in the West. The scientific opinion was that the new animal was a "panda," a name of Himalayan origin meaning "bamboo-eater." It was first used in 1825 by another French naturalist, Georges Cuvier, to describe the smaller red panda. Several expeditions were sent to western China and neighboring Tibet in search of it, but it was fifty years before any Westerner saw a live one. Although the expeditions reported seeing signs of pandas, and were given information about them by the mountain tribesmen, not once did they see a living animal. Panda skins continued to reach the West via missionaries who had purchased them from native hunters, but it was soon believed that the panda was extinct.

But the panda was not extinct. It still survived in the bamboo forests just as it had for so many years, and the searchers were eventually successful. Lieutenant J. W. Brooke who explored panda country early this century may have been the first Westerner to see one in the wild. Or it could have been General G. E. Pereira or J. H. Edgar, who both claimed to have seen a white bear in a tree. None returned with proof and Brooke was killed in 1920 by the hill tribesmen known as the Lolos. There is no doubt that the members of the Stoetzner expedition of 1916 saw a live panda, for in addition to acquiring the skins and carcasses of five pandas they also obtained a baby which expedition member Hugo Weigold attempted to raise, but failed for lack of the proper food. Now that it was certain the panda still survived, and as the early years of the century were the heyday of the big game hunter, the race was on to be the first to shoot a panda.

In 1928 Theodore and Kermit Roosevelt, sons of United States President Teddy Roosevelt, set off to China intent on shooting a panda. Their expedition was sponsored by Chicago's Field Museum of Natural History, and their search took them to the Moupin district of Sichuan where Pere David had obtained his panda specimens sixty years earlier. They were hampered in their attempts by the steep and slippery slopes, the denseness of the bamboo forest, the panda's elusiveness, and the lack of cooperation from the hill tribesmen. Despite dire warnings they eventually entered Lololand where Brooke had been murdered a few years before. After an initial period of coolness and suspicion the previously inhospitable Lolos actually helped them to locate a panda. On April 13th, 1929 near Yehli, south of the Tung River in eastern Sikang, the Roosevelt brothers fired simultaneously, as agreed before they left America, and killed a panda as it sleepily left its den in the bole of a large tree and stood yawning outside. So they were both credited with being the first Westerners to kill a panda, a feat heightened in those days by the animal's rarity. Today, just a half century later, the killing of rare animals is contrary to general world opinion.

Western envy was aroused when the Roosevelts' panda and another bought from native hunters were exhibited in the Field Museum. In 1931 the Philadelphia Academy of Natural Sciences mounted an expedition to

The first panda shot by Westerners, by Theodore and Kermit Roosevelt in 1928, is included in this diorama at Chicago's Field Museum of Natural History.

Sichuan. It was led by Brooke Dolan. In Wassu, a mountainous principality west of the Min River, the expedition encountered its first panda and one of the members, Ernst Schaefer, earned the distinction of being the third Westerner to kill one. It was just a baby, which he shot out of the branches of a tree, and its body was small enough to tuck under his arm. Later he saw three others in trees, luckily for them out of range and inaccessible. So the panda's habit of climbing trees, which probably evolved to help it escape wild dogs, was no protection at all against the

guns of modern hunters and museum collectors who in fact used their own dogs to tree the pandas.

At about the same time Floyd "Tangier" Smith led another Field Museum expedition into the mountains and returned with the bodies of two pandas that he had purchased from native hunters. Then Jack Young, who was a member of the earlier Roosevelt expedition, mounted his own search and returned with two panda skins, also both acquired from hunters. One of these skins was sent to New York's American Museum of Natural History, and in 1934 the Museum's Dean Sage expedition visited western Sichuan to collect more pandas for that institution. The expedition gathered a large collection of unique biological specimens, including the golden monkey, Styan's panda, and the blood pheasant. But the real prize eluded them. They set spear traps, hunted with dogs, and spent many days clambering up the icy slopes and sliding down them, and floundering through bamboo groves deep in snow. Two of the four Western members of the expedition were incapacitated. Donald Carter suffered a heart attack and left the high country for a camp lower down the mountainside, and Sage's wife Anne sustained a leg injury.

On November 8th, 1934, Sage and William Sheldon were searching the bamboo ridges above the Mamogo Valley when their hunters startled a panda which set off down the slope with the dogs in hot pursuit. Sage fired twice when he saw it heading towards him, but his bullets had no effect. He fired again and missed and his rifle was empty. But because the panda's movements are slow and it was just walking rapidly towards him he had time to take a cartridge from his gunbearer, load, and fire again when the panda was only three meters away. From farther up the slope Sheldon fired simultaneously at the same bear, and the third panda killed by Westerners rolled down the mountainside and came to rest in the bamboo. Sage recorded later in his diary, "We were both so overjoyed we practically had hysterics on the spot, and jumped around like loons, screaming ourselves hoarse." Their victim was an old female which they thought was a nursing mother, and with the benefit of time and knowledge it is now known that this was the right season for baby pandas. In his book *The Wilderness Home of the Giant Panda* published forty years later, Sheldon says "since the event I often wake up at night and ask myself why I did not have the presence of mind to backtrack this old female and discover where she had been when the dogs started her."

The Western world did not have to rely entirely upon mounting major expeditions to get pandas for their museum collections. The missionaries were very helpful. One in particular, David Graham, sent fifteen skins and skeletons to Washington DC's United States National Museum between 1929 and 1942. When the liberation of China brought an end to the international panda trade, the skins, skeletons, and carcasses of sixty-eight pandas had been exported. Long before then, beginning in the early 1930s, thoughts began to turn from museum dioramas to zoo cages and the race began to be the first to acquire a live panda.

The term "panda-monium" was coined to describe scenes of excitement when the first panda, Su-Lin, was exhibited in the West.

Coveting the Panda

4

While the world's museums were actively seeking panda skins and bones to mount displays in their cabinets and dioramas, zoological gardens also began to appreciate the panda's exhibition value and they made plans to acquire live ones. As was the case in the acquisition of museum specimens, if you wanted pandas you went to China to get your own, and in 1934 two Americans, Tangier Smith and William Harkness Jr., planned to do just that. Smith, who had earlier collected several skins for museums, was a Shanghai banker turned big game hunter and explorer. Harkness was a New Yorker who planned to catch a panda for the Bronx Zoo. Two weeks before he sailed for Shanghai he married a New York dress designer, but she did not accompany him and as fate would have it, never had another opportunity. For after spending a frustrating year in China, Harkness mysteriously died without ever reaching the bamboo forests. Tangier Smith, who had been waiting in Sichuan for him, then returned to Shanghai where he eventually met Mrs. Harkness when she arrived there, determined to fulfil her husband's dream of taking the first live panda to America. She tried to recruit Smith, but he was not interested in helping a novice, and a woman at that, to catch the first panda. So he returned on his own to Sichuan, where he had left his hunters who had been searching for pandas in his absence.

Ruth Harkness was forced to make her own expedition. It was that or return to New York. She headed for Sichuan accompanied by Quentin Young, the American-Chinese brother of Jack Young who had been a member of the 1928 Roosevelt expedition. Her destination was the mountainous principality of Wassu, where in the small town of Tsaopo the members of the Dean Sage expedition had headquartered in the Prince's palace two years earlier. They established camps in the mountains, questioned native hunters, and set traps. On the morning of November 9th, 1936, Ruth Harkness set off with Quentin Young and the hunters to inspect the traps, but the snow, rain, and precipitous slopes made progress very difficult. At times she had to crawl along on her hands and knees. Ahead of her the hunters startled an adult panda and began shooting at it as they all disappeared into the bamboo leaving Mrs. Harkness and Young behind.

Young, after listening intently, went over to a huge rotting tree. "From the dead tree came a baby's whimper," wrote Mrs. Harkness. "I must have been momentarily paralyzed, for I didn't move until Quentin came

Su-lin was the first live panda to visit the Western world. She was exhibited in Chicago's Brookfield Zoo in 1937 and died there in 1938.

towards me and held out his arms. There in the palms of his hands was a squirming baby beishung." Keeping the baby panda warm tucked inside Young's shirt they hurried back to their base camp to prepare a bottle. Mrs. Harkness thought the cub was a female and named her Su-lin. Since she weighed just one and a half kilograms and was still blind she was thought at the time to be about ten days old. From the experience gained since then with captive pandas, it is more likely that Su-lin was a month old when she was found.

This was the Harkness version of how the first live panda was acquired in Sichuan. The Tangier Smith story was quite different. His account of Su-lin's capture, related in a BBC radio broadcast in 1937, was that he had acquired three live pandas. The first of these was a baby which had been brought to his camp at Tsaopo while he was away. Several days later a party of travelers arrived in the neighborhood and the baby panda was sold to them for cash.

Was either Tangier Smith or Ruth Harkness telling the whole truth about Su-lin's capture, or were they both on the level, for Quentin Young could have set the whole thing up unknown to Mrs. Harkness. In their book *Men and Pandas,* Ramona and Desmond Morris believe Smith. They suggest that it was unlikely that a complete novice, as Ruth Harkness was, would find and capture a live panda within a few days of arriving in the mountains, especially since professional animal collectors such as Smith and his hunters had been trying for months. But it was the native hunters and their dogs who generally found the pandas anyway, not the Westerners they were working for, whether novice or professional. With regard to the timing, that was probably just good fortune, for finding pandas at all seemed to rest upon luck. The more important consideration involves how an immature cub could have survived for the several days Smith said it was in his camp during his absence, before the travelers arrived and purchased it.

There is no question about who brought the first live panda to the Western world. It was Harkness. However, who really caught Su-lin will remain another of the mountain's mysteries. Su-lin might not have been the first to leave China's shores anyway, if the account of the two shipped to Japan in 685 AD is correct. But transporting them alive across China to the coast and then shipping them to Japan would have been a tremendous task in those days.

Ruth Harkness finally had her panda, but it was certainly not the end of her problems. In fact, they now began in earnest. She was faced with the difficulties of returning to Shanghai and feeding the baby at regular intervals throughout the day and night, of being pestered continually by reporters and photographers, of getting permission to export Su-lin, and of arranging passages for them both. A new term "panda-monium" was coined by reporters to describe the scenes at Shanghai airport when Mrs. Harkness and Su-lin arrived there, and it was with great relief that they eventually sailed for the United States aboard the *President McKinley.*

The steamer docked at San Francisco on December 18th, 1936, and at the age of approximately ten weeks Su-lin was carried onto American soil, the first panda to reach the West alive. America went wild, according her an unprecedented reception. After a short stay in San Francisco, Mrs. Harkness and Su-lin set off for the east coast by train. On arrival at Chicago, Edward Bean, the director of the city's Brookfield Zoo, tried to persuade her to leave the panda in his care, but she insisted on continuing her journey to New York. Her reception at the Bronx Zoo, however, was a severe disappointment, for zoo officials were not keen on acquiring Su-lin after all, questioning her condition and chances of survival and expressing concern about getting adequate supplies of bamboo.

In readiness for Su-lin's weaning from baby foods onto solids Mrs. Harkness had brought back samples of bamboo for identification, as it was important to know which species were acceptable to pandas. Even back then she was not allowed to import it until all the soil had been washed off the roots. The Bronx Zoo officials were unimpressed and rejected Su-lin. This is strange considering that William Harkness had made his fatal journey to China to get them a panda and had previously mounted an expedition to the Dutch East Indies to catch Komodo dragons, the world's largest lizards, for them. Upset by the Bronx Zoo's attitude, Mrs. Harkness went back to Chicago, and on February 8th, 1937, Su-lin was safely installed at the Brookfield Zoo, the first panda ever to be exhibited in a zoological garden. The purchase price was apparently the financing of another expedition to China for more pandas, especially a young male as a mate for Su-lin.

On her second expedition Mrs. Harkness took much longer to find a panda. She went to the principality of Wassu again, and after three months acquired two cubs, but both were females. She brought one of these, first named Diana and later Mei Mei, back to the Brookfield Zoo as a companion for Su-lin. Their companionship was short-lived, for Su-lin died when a piece of wood lodged in her throat just six weeks after Mei Mei's arrival. Her loss was even more disturbing when the autopsy showed that she was in fact a male, and for just six weeks the Brookfield Zoo had actually owned a pair of pandas, or so they thought at the time. When Mei Mei died in 1942 they discovered they had been wrong again, for she was a male also.

The *International Studbook for the Giant Panda* records Tangier Smith making the third exportation of a live panda from China in 1937. To avoid publicity he dyed it dark brown to resemble a brown bear. But he could have saved himself the trouble. It died aboard the *SS Andre Lebon* between Hong Kong and Singapore en route to London. Smith was an agent for Chicago's Field Museum and had collected animals in the mountains west of Chengdu for several years, acquiring over ten thousand mammal and bird specimens for the museum. He was certainly the greatest panda collector of all time, but not the most successful. He collected a total of thirteen pandas, but only managed to deliver five of them to the London Zoo in 1938. One of those died soon after arrival, as Smith did himself, from tuberculosis. This major shipment of pandas from the Sichuan mountains to London was made with great difficulty, and as Smith was very sick at the time his wife transported the pandas by road from Chengdu to Hong Kong, a journey that took twenty-five days. En route the truck ran off the road and overturned, allowing two of the pandas to

Opposite
Ming was one of five
pandas delivered to the
London Zoo by the
animal collector Tangier
Smith in 1938. She
outlived the others and
died in 1944.

Below
Pan dee and Pan dah,
gifts from Chiang Kai-
shek, were received by
the Bronx Zoo in 1941
during the height of
World War II hostilities.

escape. They were quickly caught, but when the pandas arrived in London the oldest member of the group, called Grandma, died in just two weeks. An autopsy revealed that she had a back injury which contributed to her death. When Sung, the second member of the group, died a year later from a spinal infection it was speculated that both were probably injured when the truck crashed on the road to Hong Kong. The third panda, Happy, went to live at the St. Louis Zoo after touring Europe for a few months. Despite his name he survived, mateless, for just seven years. Tang, the fourth member of the unfortunate Smith troop of pandas, fared even worse and died in 1940. Ming survived until 1944.

The unprecedented arrival in England of five pandas in one shipment made 1938 the most active year ever in the captive history of the panda. In addition, the Bronx Zoo received Pandora through the efforts of missionary Frank Dickinson, and as a result of an exchange between the universities of New York and Chengdu, the latter received scientific equipment and books. The following year was also a good one, this time for the United States. The Brookfield Zoo finally acquired a male mate for Mei Mei (who was still believed to be a female), through the efforts of A. T. Steele, a *Chicago Daily News* correspondent. He had earlier claimed that pandas were really very common in China and that the Western world had been duped in order to increase the publicity value of the few it had received. When challenged to prove this, it took him eighteen months to get the Brookfield Zoo their third panda, Mei Lan.

Also in 1939 the Bronx Zoo received Pan and the St. Louis Zoo acquired the only two it has ever exhibited — Happy after his European tour and Pao Pei direct from China. Then, because of the Japanese occupation of China and the onset of World War II, the supply of pandas to the West dried up. With the exception of Pan dee and Pan dah, which the Bronx Zoo received as gifts from the Chinese government, no pandas came to the West. Zoo official, John Tee-Van, arrived with Pan dee and Pan dah in December 1941, making a round trip of thirty-five thousand miles to avoid the war zones, although he did fly over Japanese-held territory at one stage. During the war years Pan dee and Pan dah supplied much quiet, escapist pleasure to New Yorkers anxious to have their minds taken off the grimmer matters of the early forties.

When World War II ended, the Governor of Sichuan promised the London Zoo two pandas as a goodwill gesture from China to Britain. Dr. Ma Teh, a Chengdu University lecturer, was given the task of capturing them and taking them to England, in return for a year's study there. Even with two hundred people involved in the search it was two months before a young panda was captured. They called her Lien Ho, and she arrived in London in May 1946. For four months Dr. Ma Teh's collectors searched for a mate for Lien Ho, but they were unsuccessful and she remained by herself for the four years she lived at the London Zoo.

The live panda export business was nowhere near as successful as the earlier trade in bodies. Only fifteen pandas had been exported alive from China up to the time the communists took control, and then the supply came to an almost complete stop for twenty-five years, at least to zoos in non-communist countries. There was just one exception — the famous

Chu-lin, right, seen here with her mother, Shao Shao, at the Madrid Zoo, was the first panda born in Europe. Chi Chi, below, arrived at London Zoo in 1958 and despite a visit to Moscow where she was rebuffed by An An, she remained mateless until she died in 1972.

Chi Chi, who was exchanged for several rhinos, giraffes, hippos, and zebras supplied by Austrian animal dealer Heini Demmer. The journey from China took Demmer and Chi Chi first to Moscow Zoo, then to both the East and West zoos of Berlin, and finally to the Frankfurt Zoo for short visits, prior to them going to America. But Chi Chi was denied entry because the United States government did not recognize the communist regime in China. Trade was therefore prohibited and an exception was not made even for a panda.

After a short visit to Copenhagen Chi Chi then went to London, initially for a three-week stay. Her travels finally ended in September 1958 when the London Zoo decided to keep her, and with financial assistance from Granada TV, Chi Chi was purchased from Demmer for about £10,000. A few years earlier zoo officials had publicly announced that they would never exhibit pandas again. Their experience with Lien Ho who was a withdrawn, morose animal had been unfortunate, and the animal's confinement had been severely criticized by the national press. But since they had not been responsible for removing Chi Chi from the wild, zoo officials speculated that no criticism would be given to the zoo and therefore they had no qualms about keeping her.

It was during this period that China's zoos began to acquire their first pandas, beginning with the arrival of three in Beijing in 1955, although both Shanghai and Chengdu had one each for short periods some years before. But apart from Chi Chi the only other pandas to leave China between 1946 and 1971 went to communist countries. Moscow Zoo received two males as gifts from Mao Tse Tung to the Russian people; Ping Ping arrived first in 1957, followed by An An in 1959. Discounting an unsubstantiated report that Pere David sent a live panda to Paris, the Moscow Zoo pandas were claimed to be the first to appear on permanent display in Europe. Then, between 1965 and 1971 four pandas were sent to the zoo in Pyongyang, North Korea.

For all but three months of her fourteen-year captive life span, until 1972 when two pandas arrived at Washington DC's National Zoo, Chi Chi was the only panda on exhibit in the Western world. When she died on July 22nd, 1972, she set a longevity record, beating by a few days the zoo life span of Brookfield's Mei Lan. By coincidence the second wave of pandas to leave China, the detente phase, began the very year Chi Chi died, and signified an end to China's reluctance to associate with the West. As a result of United States President Nixon's visit to China and the reinstatement of diplomatic relations between the two countries, Hsing Hsing and Ling Ling were given to the United States and have been kept ever since at the National Zoo in Washington DC. They were the first pandas to arrive in America since Pan dee and Pan dah in 1941, and the only living specimens on display there for almost twenty years since Mei Lan died in Chicago in 1953.

In this second phase of panda exports China gave sixteen specimens to seven countries between 1972 and 1982. They were all official gifts that went to the United States, France, England, Japan, West Germany, Mexico, and Spain. Chi Chi was replaced during this period by a pair that arrived in 1974, a few months after Prime Minister Edward Heath's visit

FIGURE 1.

Pandas exported alive from China for permanent exhibition

NAME	SEX	ZOO	DATE OF ARRIVAL	DATE OF DEATH
Su-lin	M	Brookfield	1937	1938
Mei Mei	M	Brookfield	1938	1942
?	F	Died en route		1937
Pandora	F	New York	1938	1941
Ming	F	London	1938	1944
Tang	M	London	1938	1940
Sung	M	London	1938	1939
Grandma	F	London	1938	1939
Happy	M	St. Louis	1939	1946
Pao Pei	F	St. Louis	1939	1952
Mei Lan	M	Brookfield	1939	1953
Pan	M	New York	1939	1940
Pan dee	F	New York	1941	1945
Pan dah	M	New York	1941	1951
Lien Ho	M	London	1946	1950
Ping Ping	M	Moscow	1957	1961
Chi Chi	F	London	1958	1972
An An	M	Moscow	1959	1972
Lan Lan	F	Tokyo	1972	1979
Kang Kang	M	Tokyo	1972	1980
Ling Ling	F	Washington	1972	
Hsing Hsing	M	Washington	1972	
Li Li	M	Paris	1973	1974
Yen Yen	M	Paris	1973	
Ching Ching	F	London	1974	1985
Chia Chia	M	London	1974	
Pe Pe	M	Mexico City	1975	1988
Ying Ying	F	Mexico City	1975	
Chang Chang	M	Madrid	1978	
Shao Shao	F	Madrid	1978	1983
Huan Huan	F	Tokyo	1980	
Bao Bao	M	West Berlin	1980	
Tian Tian	F	West Berlin	1980	1984
Fei Fei	M	Tokyo	1982	

In addition, four pandas were exported to Pyongyang, North Korea, between 1965 and 1971. It is not known if they are still alive.

to China. Canada was one of the few major Western nations not to receive pandas, despite requests and having several zoos capable of providing the necessary accommodation and care. The phase ended soon after the signing of the World Wildlife Fund's agreement with China on panda conservation. It had lasted ten years, exactly the same as phase one, excluding the unique arrangement that involved Chi Chi.

The National Zoo's pair raised to nine the number of pandas ever exhibited permanently in North America. The only other zoos to have them were New York, St. Louis, and Brookfield which had the misfortune to own three males. In England only the London Zoo has exhibited pandas. It has had eight since 1938, although one of them was not purchased and died soon after arrival, still owned by Tangier Smith. In Europe, apart from brief visits to several zoos by Happy who eventually went to St. Louis, and Chi Chi who ended up in London, there were no pandas on permanent display until 1957 when Moscow received Ping Ping. Outside Russia there were none until the second wave of arrivals included pandas for Paris and Berlin. No others are likely to join them permanently unless China agrees to long-term breeding loans with selected Western zoos. But the chances of this happening may have been undermined by the West's continued criticism of China's conservation policies and efforts, and the poor breeding success in the West. The present total of seventeen pandas in the West should increase, or at least hold its own, as longevity rates improve and cubs are born occasionally. But the chances of breeding success rest solely on the zoos in Washington, Tokyo, and Mexico City.

The third phase of panda exports from China began in 1984 when the Los Angeles Zoo received a pair on loan to celebrate The Games of the XXI Olympiad. The new arrivals did not help Western breeding efforts. Their stay outside China was too short and was complicated by agreements that prevented breeding attempts. It was the beginning of a practice that would involve the panda and China in more dissention than all the previous controversies. But before it began, there was another significant happening in the life and times of the panda. The argument about its origin was finally settled.

Following page
Pere Armand David considered the panda to be a bear because of its bear-like appearance.

Bear or Raccoon

5

Fossils of animals that looked like the pandas of today have been found only in deposits dating since the early Pleistocene period, about two million years ago. Consequently the long-held belief is that the panda must have developed rather quickly from its immediate ancestor and is therefore the product of rapid evolution. Despite this thinking, the panda's early ancestors can be traced back to at least sixty million years to when the first carnivorous mammals began to appear on earth. These were small creatures known as Miacids, which branched out to produce the cats, dogs, bears, and other carnivores of the modern age. The traditional theory is that the dog branch split in two directions. One group evolved into the swift, intelligent hunters we know as dogs, wolves, and foxes. The other produced the ancestors of the bears and the raccoons. This branch then also split into two, one of its sub-branches evolving into today's bears, the other into the raccoons and their relative the red panda.

Which of these two branches gave rise to the panda? Supporters of a more recent theory believe that the main branch of the early carnivores split into two groups, one giving rise to the dogs and the other to the raccoons. From the dog branch evolved three separate offshoots, which became the bears, the panda, and the red panda. None of these has close ties to the raccoon at all. Was this the true origin of the panda? Since skins and skeletons of this controversial animal first reached the Western world over a century ago zoologists have debated this question.

Many distinguished scientists believed pandas developed from the bears between ten and thirty million years ago. But their equally eminent colleagues thought they branched off from the raccoon line, and the controversy has been one of the most hotly argued zoological issues of all time. It began when Professor Alphonse Milne-Edwards of Paris's Natural History Museum examined the panda material sent from China by Pere David. The new animal certainly resembled a bear, but the structure of its teeth and bones indicated that it was more closely related to the smaller red panda and therefore to the raccoons, than to the living bears. So he named it *Ailuropoda* because its feet resembled those of the red panda *Ailurs,* and this is still the panda's scientific name or genus.

Ray Lankester, director of the British Museum's Natural History department, agreed with Milne-Edwards that the skull, leg, and foot bones of the new black and white bear differed from those of the other bears and more closely resembled the red panda. Taxonomist Richard

> The panda gradually evolved from a carnivore and now restricts its diet to large quantities of bamboo.

Many taxonomists agreed with Pere David that the panda was a relative of the grizzly bear.

Lydekker also agreed that this new animal was not a bear but another form of panda. As there was already a red panda the common name of "great panda" was agreed upon, but this was soon changed to "giant panda," for it certainly was a giant by comparison to the red panda. So the panda was officially given its own place within the raccoon family, but the debate on its origin continued. The raccoon theory remained the belief of many English and American zoologists, whereas European scientists generally believed in the bear-origin theory.

Outwardly the panda resembles a bear more than it resembles any other animal, but does this mean that it is a bear? Pere David had no doubts, even though he was familiar with the red panda and had collected specimens himself. He called the panda the black and white bear. The Chinese were never in doubt either, for their various names for the panda over the years generally included "bear." First there was beishung, which translates to white bear. Then at one time they called it the banded bear, then bear cat, and now Daxiongmao (Dash wing may oh) the great bear cat. The most surprising aspect of these names however is the inclusion of "cat," for the panda is not at all cat-like.

The Chinese and Pere David had neither the benefit of comparative anatomy nor the latest knowledge of developments in animal classification, so they based their decisions entirely on appearances. But looks can be deceptive, and on their own are not proof of an animal's origin or its relationship to others. Any similarities the animals may share could have occurred for reasons other than evolutionary descent. So although the panda resembles a bear this may not imply kinship. Conversely, extreme external differences do not necessarily prove that animals are unrelated. The best example of this is the hyrax, a rabbit-like animal that is the elephant's closest living relative. Externally this relationship seems ridiculous, yet the hyrax has enough hidden anatomical similarities to the elephant to prove they are kin. Many zoologists agreed with Pere David and the Chinese that the panda must surely be a bear. The two had other things in common. The shape of their brains, the structure of the bony auditory regions of their skulls, and their respiratory tracts were all similar. They were also similar in their reproductive habits, including the delayed implantation of the fertilized egg, the litter size, and the state of their newborn young.

On the other side of the argument the raccoon and red panda proponents held firm to their beliefs. They pointed out that pandas differed from the bears in the heavy structure of their jaws and their large teeth with the multiple crowns for grinding. They were also different in the development of their forepaws for manipulating bamboo, in their male reproductive organs, in the possession of scent glands and their territorial marking behavior, and in their sheep-like bleating calls. In all of these characteristics the panda resembled the red panda. The raccoon-red panda believers also reminded their colleagues that pandas differed behaviorally from the bears, especially because they do not hibernate. Their opponents countered with the view that this resulted from the panda's poor diet and inability to store fat for the winter, and was therefore an adaptation to the environment, not an inherited characteristic.

The bear faction believed that the rest of the panda's skeleton became heavily boned as a result of chewing bamboo. In retaliation the red panda and raccoon advocates wondered how the panda's eating habits could have so affected the structure of the rest of its body. They pointed out that although at first glance the panda and red panda do not look alike, the red panda minus its long tail is certainly as similar externally to the panda as the panda is to the bears. But why would this argument carry any more weight than the original theory which held that pandas were bears because they looked like them? The controversy could not be resolved.

Normally the placing of animals in their correct scientific categories is far less complicated. Taxonomists, who are zoologists who classify animals according to their relationship to other animals, do this by comparing similarities. If these result from evolutionary descent then the animals are considered related, and the relationship is known as homology. They will then correspond in structure and origin, and an organ or a part of one animal will be similar to the same organ or part of another. For example, all members of the marsupial order are implacentals, which lack a placenta to nourish their young, irrespective of whether they look more like a cat or a mouse, as some do, than a kangaroo.

Confusion often arises because animals have similarities that are not the result of having evolved from a common ancestor. The similarities happened because the animals lived in a similar environment, even on a different continent, each one adapting in the same way to its climate, food supplies, and predators in order to survive. When these adaptations occur in unrelated animals because of living in the same way it is called analogy, and the adaptations have nothing at all to do with relationship. They are merely similar in function and appearance, not in origin. Birds, bees, and bats are the best examples of analogy. They all have wings, but these are adaptations for flying and do not denote relationship.

Deciding whether the similar features of two different species resulted from homology or analogy can be difficult and may result in animals being classified incorrectly. In the case of the panda, which had characteristics of both the bears and the red pandas, taxonomists could not agree on its origin. As a result of this uncertainty zoos have erred on the side of safety when protecting their pandas from infection. Raccoons and red pandas are known to be susceptible to the diseases of both cats and dogs, especially canine and feline distemper, and are vaccinated accordingly. Bears are not. Pandas are vaccinated just to be on the safe side.

The problem in pigeonholing the panda was the red or lesser panda, which resembled it in many ways and had been discovered and classified almost fifty years earlier. If the red panda had not existed the taxonomists would probably have all agreed long ago that the panda was a bear. Since it was first described, the red panda was always considered a close relative of the raccoon. Although it was different in having more powerful jaws and teeth, and a thumb, which were all known to be related to its diet, there were enough anatomical similarities between it and the raccoon to justify the close relationship. So if the red panda was a raccoon and the newly discovered larger panda was closely related to it, then it

FIGURE 2.

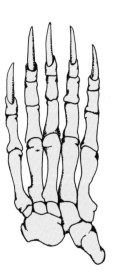
BROWN BEAR

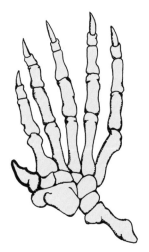
GIANT PANDA

Skeletons of the forepaws of the brown bear and the panda. Unlike the primate's thumb, which is a modified fifth digit, the panda's opposable thumb is an elongated section of its wristbone that developed for holding bamboo and not as a result of its ancestry. The thumb confused taxonomists who were attempting to classify the panda.

must also be a raccoon! Surprisingly, the reasoning that the red panda differed from the raccoon only because of its dietary adaptations was not applied by the raccoon school to the new panda controversy, for it is evident that by the same reasoning the panda could be a bear that differed from the other bears because of its diet. The raccoon school insisted, however, that the panda's similar adaptations must result from its ancestral origins, not its way of life.

Similarities in appearance were of equal value to the arguments of both sides. The panda looks like a bear and despite its reddish-brown coat the red panda looks like a raccoon, even to its banded tail. Fortunately diet is not considered to provide clues to origin or the confusion would have increased because the red panda's natural menu would suit the omnivorous bears. The red panda varies its bamboo diet with roots, fruit, berries, acorns, nuts, birds' eggs, small mammals, and even carrion, and this of course is typical bear food. But whereas the bears find this diet sufficient to deposit stores of fat for winter hibernation, the red panda remains active all winter like the panda. The debate continued until 1964 when anatomist D. Dwight Davis became convinced that the panda was a bear and attempted to prove the point in his monograph. To the belief and relief of many he finally settled the argument.

Both the panda and the red panda have opposable thumbs, as do the monkeys and apes. But the ape's thumb is a modified finger like ours, whereas Davis proved that the panda's short fat thumb is just a tough, fleshy extension of its wristbone. With this extra digit it can hold bamboo stalks and pull them to within reach of its mouth, giving it a degree of opposability approaching that of the higher mammals. Otherwise it has

bears' paws. So the panda's thumb was a clear-cut case of analogy or convergence, where both the red panda and the panda had developed thumbs for the same purpose. It was just an improvement to help a bear eat bamboo and did not imply evolutionary relationship at all.

Davis believed what had been suggested before — that the panda's slow, ambling gait and front-heavy appearance were not adaptations to its environment but had occurred as side effects of the jaw and face strengthening from chewing the hard bamboo canes. He believed that the slowness and front-heaviness were not suppressed in evolution because the panda was neither a hunter nor hunted and therefore did not need to move swiftly or agilely, or wander far in search of food. Some zoologists were still unconvinced and questioned Davis' findings on the basis that he ignored features that did not support his theories. So although his massive monograph on panda anatomy helped to swell the ranks of the bear faction the controversy persisted until recently.

In 1983 Stephen J. O'Brien and his colleagues at the National Cancer Institute, who had determined the father of the panda cub born at the National Zoo in 1983 with techniques used for settling human paternity cases, applied their expertise to the panda origin controversy. They first compared the proteins from panda cells with those of the red panda, raccoon, kinkajou, and six species of bears, basing their experiments on the 1962 "molecular clock" concept of Linus Pauling and Emile Zuckerkandl. They concluded that mutations in animal DNA — the nucleic acid that is the chief constituent of chromosomes — are inherited by future generations as isolated populations separate. They believed a comparison

FIGURE 3.

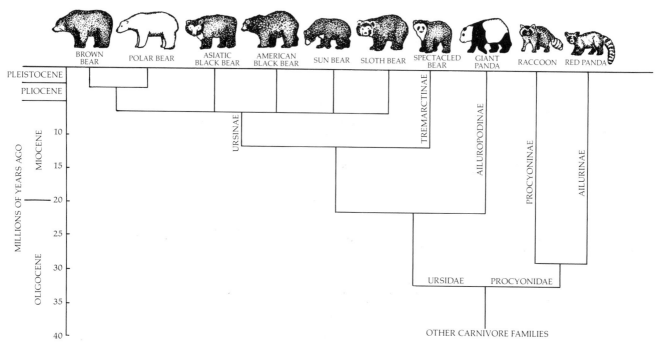

Evolutionary tree of the red panda, panda, and the bears, based on their genetic similarities and resulting from the research of Stephen J. O'Brien and his associates. The scale, in millions of years, shows when they split off from their ancestors.

of these molecular mutations should indicate relationship. Their first experiments involved culturing cells with radioactive material, which the cells absorbed as they multiplied and divided. This radioactive material was then mixed with non-radioactive cells from another species of bear.

By comparing the temperatures needed to make these cells separate it was possible to determine the degree of relationship of the animals tested. The results showed that while the cats and dogs were developing along their own lines, one branch of the ancestral carnivores gave rise to the bears and raccoons. The raccoon line then split to produce the modern-day raccoons in one group and the red panda as the sole member of the other. The bear line also split up between twenty-five and twenty million years ago to give rise to the pandas in one group and the remaining bears in the other. Not convinced, the scientists continued

their work with studies based on the techniques used to determine the paternity of the National Zoo's baby panda. By comparing enzymes from the nine other species of carnivores in the study they were able to estimate the number of mutational differences in their genes, and discovered that these varied according to the time the species had been isolated from each other. This helped to confirm their evolutionary theory.

Still unconvinced, O'Brien sought the help of David Goldman of the National Institute of Mental Health to do further research, this time involving mass protein migration when exposed to an electric field, its mobility indicating the genetic relationship. The results again confirmed the earlier findings — that pandas must have evolved from the bears. More proof of the relationship came from Vincent Sarich of the University of California when he studied the degree of immune reaction whereby systems recognize and accept or reject foreign tissue. From his findings he reached the same conclusion, that the panda is more closely related to the bears than to the raccoons. Finally it was necessary to solve one last puzzle. How could pandas be closely related to the bears when the number and shape of their chromosomes were so different? The panda has forty-two chromosomes, most of which have two arms, yet the bears have seventy-four. When William G. Nash of the National Cancer Institute compared the light and dark banding patterns of the chromosomes through the special techniques he had developed, he discovered that the patterns of the bear's chromosomes matched those on the arms of the panda's chromosomes. From this he concluded that some of the panda's chromosomes were simply bear chromosomes fused end to end.

The conclusion of all this intense research was that the panda really did evolve from the bears and not the raccoons. And the red panda, which had caused most of the confusion in the first place, is indeed a member of the raccoon family. But because both pandas diverged from their ancestors long ago, and deserve more zoological separation than different genera would indicate or provide, they should be given subfamily status in their respective families. After a century of controversy it was finally proved that the panda is a member of the Ursidae or bear family. For once external similarities were not deceptive, and were eventually supported by the required scientific data.

Another interesting discovery resulted from the work of O'Brien and his colleagues. When they compared known primate evolution with their findings and conclusions on the molecular evolution of the nine carnivores in their study, they were able to show that the panda actually split from the bears about twenty million years ago. Its development was therefore the result of gradual evolution after all, not the product of accelerated development about three million years ago as previously believed.

Vegetarian Carnivore

6

The panda and bamboo; the two are inseparable. It is a remarkable association, although there are many other animals that have specialized diets. There is an egg-eating snake, a hawk that eats only snails, one relative of the kangaroo that just eats eucalyptus leaves, and another that survives on ants and termites. But they are all rather obscure creatures, little known beyond zoological circles. The panda's dependence upon bamboo is common knowledge, and its diet is probably more widely known than that of any other animal. Since Pere David's travels in China the West has known that the panda eats bamboo, and it was even suggested since then that it eats only one kind of bamboo. However, this was disproved when two Chinese researchers discovered that pandas actually eat up to twenty-five different species of bamboo that grows in their natural habitat. The most important to them are the ones commonly known as the umbrella bamboo, arrow bamboo, and golden bamboo. The arrow bamboo is very thin, grows to about three meters tall, and resembles leafy, growing arrows, while the umbrella bamboo has a much thicker cane and grows to almost double the height. The golden bamboo is the species most often given to captive pandas, especially in North America where it is a common ornamental garden plant in temperate regions.

The panda is the most vegetarian bear, and is the only carnivore to have changed to a completely herbivorous diet in the wild, a habit that has earned it the title "monk among the carnivores" after the Buddhists who abstain from eating meat. Yet the fossil record shows that the panda was a real carnivore long ago, the same as prehistoric meat-eaters from which it evolved. Of the vegetarian panda, Ramona and Desmond Morris say "it has waved goodbye to the nimble-minded world of helter-skelter chases, bloated blood-feasts, and sprawling catnaps. Instead it has become a manual labourer, toiling endlessly at its bamboo-picking task." But as R. F. Ewer has since pointed out, this is a comparison of the panda and the exclusively predacious carnivores such as the lion or wolf which are both consumers of the big meat meal followed by several days of digesting and fasting. The most valid comparison of the panda with other carnivores is with its closer relatives the bears and the assorted members of the raccoon family. Both groups have a fondness for vegetable food and have lost the killing techniques needed for dealing with prey large enough to provide the feasts conjured up by the Morris' description.

> Because bamboo has limited nutritional value the panda does not store fat and therefore cannot hibernate during the winter.

Although almost completely dependent on bamboo in the wild, captive pandas have developed a liking for a variety of fruit and vegetation.

Why did the panda abandon a flesh diet for a vegetable one? Why would any animal forsake meat for bamboo's hard, woody stems and tough, fibrous leaves? It may have been because the early pandas were not too successful as hunters in the first place. But it is more probable that bamboo was far more plentiful and easier to get than any other food. The change happened gradually of course, over hundreds of thousands of years, and as the panda's habits changed and it became more dependent upon bamboo, the panda's shape changed also and it was less agile and less able to acquire meat, which in turn increased its dependency on bamboo. Today's pandas cannot chase large animals and despatch them in the same way that the wolves and wild dogs do, but neither can the other northern bears, with the exception of the polar bear, yet they did not become total vegetarians.

The three northern species of terrestrial bears — the American black, the Himalayan black, and the brown bear — are basically omnivorous and occupy the same environmental zone as the panda. Unlike the single-minded panda they prefer variety and have a definite seasonal cycle of food sources. When they break out of their hibernation dens in spring appearing gaunt and scruffy they eat roots, bulbs, grass, and other plant life and dig up rodents. In summer they eat berries and the eggs and young of ground-nesting birds, and in the autumn they eat nuts and acorns and congregate at salmon runs to gorge on the spawning fish. They eat carrion whenever they can, either animals that have died naturally or the leftovers of other predators' meals. When the opportunity exists they kill domestic animals, especially sheep and goats, and they raid crops and campsites.

The bulk of the northern land bears' hunting, if it can be called that, is restricted to digging rodents out of their burrows. They leave a trail of overturned stones, ripped-open logs, and opened-up burrows in their search for invertebrates and ground squirrels. But watchers report no such signs along panda trails. William Sheldon, who spent several months stalking pandas in the Sichuan mountains, never saw any signs to indicate that pandas had been digging for rodents or even searching for insects. In all the more recent observations of pandas and their behavior there is just one account of a panda digging like a bear to open up rodents' burrows. This was the sighting by Pen Hung Shou on the Tibetan plateaus. But Western zoologists believe the animals Pen saw, at a great distance, were probably pale-colored Tibetan brown bears. Pen was also told by local tribesmen that the panda caught fish, just as the American brown bears do, but this has never been confirmed by other observers.

Although the bamboo forests of western China harbor large numbers of mouse-sized voles and shrews, they do not have the colonies of burrowing and hibernating ground squirrels and marmots that are common in North America. If they did, and it was the panda's habit to hunt them, they would soon be exterminated, for the panda's small range compared to the huge territory of the brown bear could not support such activities for long. The only terrestrial rodent of the bamboo zone equivalent to North America's ground squirrels in size is

Opposite
The pandas differ from
the bears in their ability
to grasp and chew
bamboo.

the bamboo rat, a mole-like animal that tunnels under the bamboo and like the panda eats little else. Heaving mounds of soil above the surface, as real moles do, the bamboo rat ventures above ground only to gnaw off the stems that are its main diet. At such a time it would be vulnerable to a panda sitting quietly in the same clump of bamboo. But there is only one record of a panda catching and eating a mole rat.

Despite living on bamboo for so long and becoming completely dependent upon it in the wild, the panda never forgot that it was really a carnivore and it is still an opportunist when there is a chance of a meat meal. But with little hope of catching its own prey it must rely on carrion. The remains of various creatures from golden monkeys to musk deer have been found in pandas' stomachs, although very rarely. As it would be virtually impossible for pandas to catch these themselves, they must have come across the remains of animals that had died naturally or were killed by the real predators. Pere David was therefore correct in believing that the panda ate other foods, but he was wrong when he said it must be carnivorous in winter. Pandas seldom miss an opportunity to scavenge meat in the wild as workers in the Fengtongzai Reserve which adjoins Wolong discovered when they threw bones into the bush behind their camp. Wild pandas were quick to locate this source of their second most favorite food and came regularly looking for handouts. Scientists have also taken advantage of this knowledge and baited their traps with meat to catch pandas for radio-collaring.

So the panda has definitely retained its carnivorous ancestor's craving for meat, unlike the true vegetarians such as the leaf-eating colobus monkey and the fruit-eating flying fox or giant fruit bat, which never eat meat. Pandas are virtually complete vegetarians in the wild through the lack of opportunity rather than desire. Their meat-eating opportunities are obviously very infrequent and compared to the rest of its diet, the amount of meat eaten by a free-roaming panda is insignificant. To all intents and purposes the wild panda is a pure vegetarian, a bamboo-eating bear, whose day is spent either steadily chewing bamboo to produce the energy needed to sustain it or resting to conserve that energy.

Several other carnivores abandoned their pure meat diet for an omnivorous one as they evolved. Most of the bears did, as did the kinkajous, raccoons, and their relatives; and so did some of the wild dogs such as the raccoon dog and the gray fox that eat acorns, berries, fruit, and grain as well as meat. Yet going a step farther and becoming mainly a vegetarian as are the red panda, South America's spectacled bear, and the Malayan sun bear, was unusual. To refine this adaptation to its extreme and become dependent upon one kind of plant, as the panda has, is unique. But even when the changes that occurred as it slowly stopped hunting made it difficult or impossible for the panda to catch any significant numbers of animals, it could still have relied on a more varied diet as did the black and brown bears. Yet there are no records of pandas eating acorns or berries, and when they do roam above the tree line to the mountain meadows they do not take advantage of the nutritious bulbs and herbs growing there. On the few occasions their droppings

have been seen in the alpine zone they still contained only the remains of bamboo meals.

Pandas do eat some of the other plants growing in the bamboo zone, such as horsetails, rushes, aster, wild parsnip, the bark of conifers, and the leaves of willow, bramble, and other deciduous trees and shrubs. Their intake of these is insignificant, however, and 99 percent of their diet is bamboo. They are completely dependent upon it, and the ultimate proof of this was provided during the bamboo die-off emergencies. Although the pandas' consumption of other vegetation increased it could not sustain them and many died of starvation.

Why has the panda become so dependent upon bamboo? Mainly because in winter a variety of food is scarce and the other available evergreens do not appeal to it. Although it does eat small amounts of juniper and spruce needles, there are no records of the panda eating rhododendron leaves, the most plentiful evergreen higher up the slopes. Bamboo itself is not exactly ever green, as many leaves die during the winter although they remain on the stems until spring. The protein content of these is much lower than for the fresh green ones but is still higher than the green stems that are also available. There is very little other food for the panda in winter. The grass is dead, the deciduous leaves have fallen, and deep snow covers all the ground vegetation. Despite its poor nutritional value, there is no better food than bamboo.

Bamboo has two advantages over most grasses and other vegetation. No other food item in western China's mountains is more plentiful and available year-round, even in winter when several feet of its length are buried in the snow. But bamboo became the panda's nemesis. As its dependency developed the panda could not hibernate as do the other northern bears. Its nutritionally poor diet did not provide the fat resources needed to sleep for five months. For most hibernators, hibernation results from the seasonal lack of food, not the inability to withstand cold. While the other bears were snug in their underground dens because their regular food was no longer available, and they had stored enough fat anyway, the need for more bamboo forced the panda to roam the snow-clad trails all winter.

The layer of fat that northern bears accumulate by late autumn can be up to fifteen centimeters thick on their hips. It allows them to sleep the winter away in a den where their cubs are born. This is a different kind of hibernation to the ground squirrels and the dormice whose body temperatures drop to just above freezing point. Animals in that condition could not give birth and raise their young. Bears are different.

FIGURE 4.

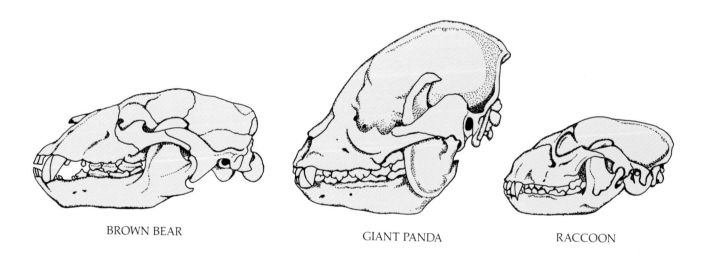

BROWN BEAR   GIANT PANDA   RACCOON

Skulls of the brown bear, panda, and raccoon showing the tremendous enlargement of the panda's cranium and its massive teeth, which evolved to provide the grinding power needed to eat the bamboo's tough stems and leathery leaves.

Although they are inactive in their dens and their rates of breathing and heartbeat are lowered, their body temperatures drop little below normal. Inactivity does not use up much energy and a fat bear can survive all winter, even converting its waste product urea back into protein, and providing milk for up to three cubs.

On a diet of bamboo the panda can do none of these things. Its day is only just long enough to eat all the bamboo needed to nourish it, and there is no energy left for storage. If the panda was fat enough in the autumn to stop eating as the other northern bears do, it would probably have evolved to hibernate. Possibly it did before it settled for a bamboo diet, for it has the ability to store fat, as zookeepers have discovered. Captive pandas may eat so much of their protein- and carbohydrate-rich gruel that they put on weight very quickly — a typical bear trait — and then have the means to hibernate if their physiology would allow.

Although bamboo is a nutritionally poor food it is certainly richer in nutrients than the other perennial grasses. Their growing point is just above soil level and they return their energy to the roots for storage in the fall, leaving dry brown leaves above ground for the winter. The grasses have less nutritional value than bamboo and must be dug out of the snow too, which is energy-sapping on cold days. Except after a die-off, bamboo is also close at hand, for it is not only plentiful in area but the groves are very dense, with up to eighty stems the thickness of a man's finger growing in a square meter of arrow bamboo forest. Upon waking and shaking the snow from its coat, a panda need only stretch out a hairy paw to pull down a bamboo stem, place it sideways in its mouth, and bite off a section.

If bamboo can support a large animal like the panda, if it eats enough, why are the black and brown bears not more dependent upon it? They eat bamboo shoots as well as other vegetation, so they are aware of its edibility. But because they prefer a different diet the mountains of China can support populations of three distinct species of related animals. This is nature's way of making the best possible use of the resources.

Pandas readily eat many different species of bamboo. They do not dig up the bamboo's nutritious rhizomes or underground stems, but eat everything above ground — the stems, leaves, and shoots. Their intake of each varies according to the season and the species of bamboo. Sometimes they eat stems or canes only, another time just the leaves, and in spring they eat the new shoots when these have reached a certain height.

Other vegetarians such as omnivorous humans who have voluntarily chosen a diet of plant material only, eat legumes and nuts high in plant protein, and seeds and grains rich in carbohydrates. In contrast bamboo is nutritionally poor and its value is further reduced because its bulk is made up of cellulose, the fibrous plant material that only animals with very specialized stomachs can digest. The bamboo's leaves are its most valuable food item as they contain about 15 percent protein when green and almost 10 percent when dead, and their value is increased because they have less cellulose than the woody stems. So the panda's digestive tract is filled with nutritious food when it eats leaves. But with the cellulose-rich stems its stomach is crammed with bulky, indigestible material just to get the 5 percent protein they contain.

Why then does the panda not restrict its diet to bamboo leaves? The answer is that although it obviously does not know the protein content of the bamboo it eats, it does know what is best for it. Without the bamboo canes the panda cannot slough off the excess mucous that lines its intestine to help it cope with such a coarse diet. George Schaller and Hu Jinchu estimated that an adult panda consumes between ten and eighteen kilograms of bamboo daily, eating slightly more stems than leaves on an annual basis. Pandas eat so much that often they almost clear-cropped a small area when they remained in the same grove for long periods. At other times they just snipped stems here and there as they ambled slowly along a trail.

The panda has become adapted to a bamboo diet to the extent that its long-term survival is dependent upon it, so the other disadvantage of the bamboo, its habit of dying periodically and providing no nutrients at all, can be disastrous to the panda's way of life. Years ago the panda could overcome the loss of bamboo in one area by migrating to another. Now, with bamboo's restricted and fragmented distribution the panda may not be able to do this.

The panda's modifications to cope with bamboo are extensive, but mainly involve the adaptations needed to eat it. To chew the tough, woody bamboo canes and fibrous leaves, the evolving panda developed powerful jaw muscles and heavy jaws. And most of its forty-two teeth are large, flat premolars and molars with multiple cusps or points for grinding. To contain all of these the panda's head grew very large. If it had become extinct long ago and was known only from fossils, scientists would have been able to guess that the panda was a vegetarian from the structure of its jaws and teeth. But it is unlikely that anyone would have believed that it lived solely on bamboo.

To pull the bamboo within reach and eventually to hold it, the panda developed the equivalent of a thumb, in reality an extension of its wristbone. To cope with swallowing the coarse and spiky pieces of bamboo stem, the panda's gullet has a leathery and horny lining. Its stomach is thick-walled and very muscular, but it is single-chambered, unlike those of the other strict herbivores such as the ruminating giraffe, antelope, and cattle, and the leaf-eating monkeys called langurs. These have multiple or complicated stomachs with special bacteria to break down the cellulose, the main component of green plants, for later digestion.

Unable to digest cellulose, pandas are forced to eat large amounts of its indigestible bulk in order to derive the protein, carbohydrates, and other nutrients from the plant cells. A grass-eating ruminant digests up to 80 percent of its food, but the panda can only digest about 30 percent of its intake.

To absorb the sparse nutrients from its unusual diet the panda still has the short gut of the carnivore, despite living on bamboo for so long. In fact, its intestine is shorter overall than those of other carnivores the same size as the panda, and it is lined with a thick layer of mucous.

Animals that eat herbage usually have long intestines and a particularly well developed caecum or blind intestine. The koala's caecum is two meters long. But the koala is a specialized herbivore that cannot change from its pure vegetarian diet. The panda is a carnivore that has become dependent upon bamboo through circumstance, and despite being a vegetarian by dietary adaptation is basically still a carnivore with vegetarian tendencies. The koala never was a carnivore.

The shortening of the panda's gut has occurred mostly in the section immediately following its stomach, and it is speculated that the bamboo moves quickly through this section, where little absorption takes place anyway, so that it arrives all the sooner in the lower gut where the assimilation of nutrients occurs. Food passes through this type of digestive system very quickly, and the end result of such large meals of indigestible food is a tremendous output of droppings, which look like compacted packages of bamboo stalk. This bulk is necessary for the panda's system as it clears out the mucous that otherwise builds up in its intestines. When full of bamboo the panda may go to sleep on the spot, without even attempting to make a nest. It just curls up and sleeps for several hours. When it arouses and wanders off to start feeding again, up to forty packages of dung may be left behind.

Practically all zoo animals receive a totally substitute or replacement diet, for it is usually impossible to provide the exact foods they eat in the wild. Anteaters readily accept raw eggs, hamburger, and milk; monkeys are given highly nutritious chow plus apples, oranges, and other fruit they would never find in their natural environment. The more exacting herbivores such as the leaf-eating giraffe-necked antelope are given the finest alfalfa hay, whereas bison and pronghorn that graze the coarse grasses of the prairies receive less nutritious fare. For the panda there is no substitute vegetation, and it must have bamboo even though some captive pandas have been able to survive for a while without it.

With few exceptions bamboo has always formed the bulk of the panda's zoo diet. Yet although there has never been any serious attempt to wean them from bamboo onto other vegetation even though zoo pandas readily graze the grass in their enclosures, feeding bamboo alone has never been practised. For zoos never had any doubt about the panda's preference or need for a more nutritious diet. Since Su-lin arrived in the Brookfield Zoo in 1937, zoos have gone to extreme lengths and spared no expense to acquire fresh supplies of bamboo for their valuable guests, but they have always supplemented this with a variety of other foods. These have included fresh fruit and vegetables such as apples, carrots, cooked sweet potatoes, spinach, celery, lettuce, beet tops, and chard. All pandas have been fond of gruel, which is made of cereals rich in carbohydrates and protein such as rice, rolled oats, couscous, corn meal, and soybean flour. These are blended with powdered milk, sugar, honey, and vitamin and mineral supplements. Zoo pandas usually prefer diluted milk as their main drink and they love sugar cane. Practically all zoo pandas have also readily accepted cooked meat, and they prefer chicken to beef. The exceptions were the four pandas exhibited at the New York Zoo. They would never eat flesh in any form.

This more nutritious and concentrated diet is obviously less suitable to the panda's digestive system than its natural bulky diet of bamboo, so the panda's addiction to rich supplements can cause problems in captivity. The short-term result of such good zoo nutrition is obesity, which affects longevity and breeding potential. The captive weight record belongs to Moscow Zoo's Ping Ping who so loved his gruel that he once weighed one hundred and seventy-eight kilograms, at least fifty kilograms more than the average adult male panda. He lived only four years. The long-term result of such an unnaturally rich and concentrated diet is its effect on the panda's specialized horny gullet and the lining of its thick-walled muscular stomach. These may eventually be unable to cope with a coarse diet again. In the very long term the lack of regular and lengthy chewing would affect the panda's powerful jaws and huge teeth, which were both developed for that purpose.

But there may not be any long-term possibilities, for without sufficient bamboo the layer of mucous in the digestive tract can build up and plug the intestine. If the panda survived it would probably be so habituated to an unnatural diet that the ultimate aim of all zoo breeding — the eventual return of the endangered animal to its natural environment to live wild and free — could never be achieved. In the zoological garden the answer has been to formulate a diet composed of both bamboo and more nutritious supplements, which combines the occupational and physiological therapy of chewing bamboo for long periods with the improved nutrition needed for good health and reproduction.

The Trouble With Bamboo

7

Bamboo is a tough evergreen grass usually associated with the world's warmer regions but it is a plentiful plant in temperate climates as well. There are almost two hundred kinds of bamboo in China alone, and many of them thrive at higher elevations where their canes are half buried beneath snow for several months each year. With its shallow, mat-like root system and dense growth that deters other forms of plant life, a bamboo grove is a mass of close-packed green canes and long, tough leaves, except for the larger trees which provide the shade it prefers. Even these shade trees must become established in a clearing or during a bamboo die-off, for their seeds cannot germinate and become established in thriving bamboo groves. These are usually so dense that most animals are deterred also, except the burrowing bamboo rat and the panda. It glides easily through the canes while hunters and biologists flounder and thrash in their efforts to follow.

Bamboo normally reproduces by sending out stems called rhizomes just beneath the surface. New shoots sprout up quickly from these each spring. They grow in the manner of a telescope opening, and if conditions are favorable they reach their full height in one season. Some bamboos grow leaves in their first year also, while others wait until the following year. The stems (culms or canes) mature by increasing in hardness each year and they eventually die. But since they are being replaced annually this regular small loss causes no problems. Occasionally however, bamboo also reproduces in a completely different manner, by flowering and seeding. This causes severe problems because it then dies the next year. Luckily this does not happen very often — in some species only once a century, in others every thirty-five to forty years. When it does happen there is no mature bamboo available for the pandas for several years — until the seeds have germinated, the rhizome system has developed, and the new shoots have sprouted. As the winter climate of the mountains is harsh and the summers are quite short, the seeds may take two years to germinate. Then it is at least seven years before the canes reach their maximum height and diameter. During all this time there is no food for the pandas.

Bamboo flowerings are often synchronized over a wide area, sometimes several hundred square kilometers in extent, and every plant of the same species may flower, seed, and then die. Nobody really knows why bamboo dies en mass, but two main theories have been suggested. One is that old age and the denseness of the root mat make it necessary to

The bamboo groves in Sichuan province are subject to periodic die-offs and destruction caused by agriculture. Without bamboo the panda cannot exist.

clear the area for the next generation of bamboo. This makes more sense than the other suggestion that has been called "predator flooding." This theory suggests that animals were unable to specialize in eating bamboo seeds because they were available so infrequently. Then the bamboo suddenly produced far more than the unprepared seed-eaters could cope with. This seems rather pointless as the bamboo reproduces quite successfully between seedings through its rhizomes. Perhaps the real reason is that the poor-quality soil on the mountainsides is enriched by the rotting root mat when the bamboo dies. Whatever the reason for the well-spaced devastation of the bamboo groves, the fact that so many bamboos die off together is as mysterious as why they do it at all.

In the South American jungle or the mountains of Japan, which are both strongholds of the bamboo family, a major die-off would not cause alarm. It may in fact go unnoticed because none of the animals there is dependent upon it. But in western China two animals are totally dependent on bamboo. Although the tufted deer, golden monkey, red panda, and several other animals eat a small amount of bamboo, the bamboo rat and the panda must have it regularly. When a mass die-off of one species occurs they must find an alternate supply or starve. Bamboo rats migrate like lemmings when their food supply is interrupted, but nobody knows how successful they are in traveling the great distances needed to find another supply. Where the panda is concerned the results of a bamboo die-off are known to be dramatic and often terminal.

Bamboo has obviously been flowering, seeding, and dying periodically for many millenia and the pandas have coped with the situation or we would know them only from their fossilized bones. During their evolution they survived the temporary loss of one kind of bamboo and possibly even several kinds at one time because they could find others nearby that still flourished. Or they could migrate to another region where the bamboo was not affected. But in those days the bamboos were distributed over a much larger area since early man was a hunter and gatherer, not a farmer who cultivated the land the bamboos needed. The bamboo habitat was not fragmented by crops and forest clearance and the mountains' lower slopes were not settled and farmed as they are today. Now the bamboo is so reduced by these activities that many wild pandas can no longer migrate to other areas. Restricted to patches of suitable habitat separated by cleared and cultivated land, they could not find alternate food and when the bamboo died twice in recent years almost one fifth of all the wild pandas died also.

In western China in the mid 1970s, several species of bamboo on which the pandas relied for food — especially the umbrella bamboo — flowered, seeded, and died. This seriously depleted the already small population of wild pandas. However, this loss had one positive effect. It drew world attention to this new and serious threat to the panda and stimulated crucial conservation measures. This may not have otherwise happened. The bamboo forest of the Min Mountains where Sichuan borders Gansu province was the most seriously affected by the synchronized die-off in 1975 and 1976. At this time five thousand square kilometers of bamboo died. The umbrella bamboo was the worst casualty, and as it was the only species acceptable to the pandas in some areas they had no food at all and almost one hundred and fifty pandas are reported to have died. Even this figure may have been conservative, for in the Wanglang Reserve alone, which lies in the heart of the Min Mountains, the pandas were almost exterminated. Whereas in 1969 about two hundred were reported living there, ten years later less than twenty could be found.

There was a severe earthquake in the region during the same period which was accompanied by major landslides and this may also have killed pandas. Some of the bamboo that the pandas preferred actually survived in other parts of the Wanglang Reserve, but the pandas could not reach it in time. In the Baishuijiang Reserve, the only one in Gansu Province but still within the Min Mountains, almost all the umbrella bamboo in one section of the reserve died after flowering, yet elsewhere only half of it died. Despite this, fifty pandas are reported to have died of starvation.

The two mysteries surrounding the bamboo as a plant have yet to be solved. Why does it flower and die, and why does this normally happen in such major synchronized fashion? There is yet a third mystery that is equally puzzling. Why are some bamboo species and populations so erratic in their flowering and seeding behavior? On the same mountainside small areas of some bamboos may bloom annually, then suddenly one year the remainder bloom en mass. In other areas the same species of bamboo may die completely over a huge tract of country, yet on nearby hillsides it dies only above or below a certain elevation, followed several years later by the balance.

In the 1976 mass die-off all the umbrella bamboo in Jiuzhaigou Reserve flowered from twenty-six hundred meters to its high limit of thirty-two hundred meters. The groves below this band survived, but then flowered in 1983 down to twenty-three hundred meters, their lowest limit. By then the plants above twenty-six hundred meters had recovered so the pandas found sufficient food through moving up and down the same mountainside. In contrast the arrow bamboo in Wanglang Reserve flowered and died below twenty-nine hundred meters in the mid 1970s and then above that elevation in 1983.

Fortunately bamboo signals its impending death by flowering the year before. Some species are even more considerate for they also give an extra year's warning, signaling their intention to flower by not producing shoots the year before. In future this will allow time before the die-off instead of after, to determine if pandas should be relocated to other areas.

The bamboo crisis of the mid-seventies at least prepared China and the world for a repeat performance, which happened a few years later. In 1983 there was a mass flowering of the arrow bamboo in the Qinling and Qionglai Mountains of central Sichuan. This is the site of the Wolong Reserve that has the largest population of wild pandas. The following year 90 percent of the bamboo seeded and then died, and one quarter of the pandas in the region faced an emergency situation. Fortunately for the pandas of Wolong there were other species of bamboo available and the pandas can survive until the arrow bamboo regenerates, which it

Pandas need a
minimum of twelve
kilograms of bamboo
daily.

seems to be doing far quicker than expected. In other localized areas, however, there was no alternate food supply and sixty-two pandas died.

The final outcome of this latest bamboo crisis was not as disastrous as the first one, mainly because China was prepared for such an event. To avoid the heavy losses of the previous crisis the government sent several thousand helpers into the mountains to rescue pandas. Committees were formed in every county that was affected by the bamboo die-off to supervise the operations. They organized teams to find and rescue pandas and they built holding facilities where the pandas could be rehabilitated. The government also offered the villagers rewards for rescuing pandas, and banned the cutting of bamboo wherever pandas lived. Rescue centres were established in twenty-two counties of north-western Sichuan where pandas still survived, and six rehabilitation centres were built and staffed by veterinarians trained in panda care and treatment at the Chengdu Zoo.

As the panda habitat in Sichuan's mountains was far too large for government employees to patrol, this work was contracted to teams of peasants and forest workers. They patroled the mountains looking for sick and starving pandas, kept watch for poachers, prevented illegal forest-clearing and bamboo-shoot cutting, and kept a lookout for forest fires. They received a reward for the pandas they rescued and took their duties very seriously. There are many examples of them assisting pandas in difficulty. In Baoxin County a peasant woman cutting wood jumped into an icy river to rescue a weak panda. With help she carried it to her village where a fire was lit to warm the chilled animal. Schoolchildren in the same county drove off a dog that was attacking a panda, and then escorted it into the hills to safety.

This system of patrol and rescue teams proved very effective in saving pandas from starvation. When the crisis ended seventy pandas had been rescued, although twelve died soon afterwards. Twenty-five of the survivors were released in other areas where bamboo was still available and the remainder were kept in captivity.

There has since been criticism of the government's handling of the crisis on two counts. First, that not all of the captured pandas actually needed rescuing. Secondly, that keeping over thirty of the rescued pandas in captivity instead of rehabilitating them was excessive and more effort should have been made to find suitable wild habitat for them. Offering financial rewards for rescuing pandas in difficulty has also been questioned. Introduced during the last bamboo crisis the rescue operation still occurs even though the crisis has ended. Although efforts have apparently been made to stop the practice, the initial enthusiasm of the peasants to rescue pandas is unabated and the reward is now considered by some to be the equivalent of a live-capture bounty.

This panda at the
Chengdu Zoo was one
of the many rescued
from starvation by the
Chinese government
after the bamboo
die-off.

Conservation in the Zoo

8

There are three ways to save animals facing the immediate prospect of extinction. Leave them where they are but provide the protection and other help they need, translocate them to a safer area, or remove them to the security of captivity. Deciding the best course of action is not easy, and decisions are usually controversial and often criticized. This is certainly the case with the panda, although there are some facts that cannot be ignored. The most important is that all wild pandas obviously cannot be left in China's western mountains because their numbers are dwindling rapidly as poaching and loss of habitat take their toll.

Currently there is no planned program to translocate pandas to safer areas. It is doubtful if any region is really safe anyway since pandas are even being poached in the reserves. The captive approach is certainly the most secure one. But although captivity has been the salvation of several other endangered species, initially it may not guarantee successful breeding and long-term survival. This is currently the panda's situation, just as it was the situation of the lowland gorilla years ago. Before the first captive birth in 1956, critics claimed gorillas were impossible to breed in captivity and caging them was unjustified. Now an average of twenty-five are born annually in zoos, and their perpetuation is assured in captivity even if their chances of survival in the wild are slim. The difference between the two animals is that there always were more gorillas than pandas in zoos, and pandas are unsociable animals that do not need the regular company of their kind to thrive.

Until now the captive breeding record of pandas was not good enough to ensure their long-term survival. For this reason, plus the extreme view that a wild and free and then extinct animal is better off than a zoo specimen, there has always been opposition to captive conservation. Emphasis on captive breeding is not just the biased opinion of the zoo community. The World Wildlife Fund's position is that it is essential to the panda's survival to maintain a viable captive population, provided all specimens are included in an integrated breeding program.

Although captivity is not necessarily synonymous with conservation, the breeding successes are increasing. For years the classic cases of the survival of Pere David's deer and the European bison were cited to prove the value of captive breeding. There are many more recent achievements which include the Arabian oryx, addax, Przewalski's horse, European eagle owl, blackbuck, mikado pheasant, and the Bali mynah. Zoo-raised individuals were returned to their native lands to restock vacant or

Improved breeding programs for captive pandas would increase their numbers.

Opposite
The first captive panda
birth occurred at the
Beijing Zoo in 1963.

depleted areas. The future of two other species that faced insurmountable problems in the wild now depends entirely upon captive breeding. One is the black-footed ferret, which survives only in captivity since distemper wiped out the last of the wild ones. The other is the Californian condor. Its conservation was an example of bureaucratic and political indecision until the eleventh hour, when despite repeated requests over many years to rescue the last condors, the wild population was down to five specimens before permission was granted. The condors' survival now rests almost entirely on young raised from eggs collected in the wild a few years earlier.

Despite having a total population of between nine hundred and a thousand specimens, the panda is actually more endangered and less likely to survive than several other species with far fewer individuals. Pere David's deer, the Arabian oryx, and Przewalski's horse were all saved through captive breeding after their numbers dropped to less than twenty. Carnivores such as the endangered Siberian tiger and the Chinese leopard breed so readily in zoos that controls are now placed on their output. Even though they have recovered from near extinction, the total world populations of all these animals still number less than the panda, yet their survival is assured. This is because they breed more readily in captivity than the panda does, which is true of so many mammals. The immediate benefit of captive conservation is the protection given to the species from predators, poachers, and natural hazards such as food shortages and loss of habitat. But if the pandas do not reproduce faster than their attrition rate there is obviously no advantage. Contrarily it is only through study, research, and experimentation with confined pandas that the breeding problems will be overcome.

The productivity of captive pandas in China is still mediocre, although it continues to get better. But the captive-raising record, by both mother and surrogate, needs much improvement. Initially Chinese zoos fared worse than the West in acquiring pandas for exhibition. Apart from two short-lived individuals in Shanghai and Chengdu, it was not until 1955 that the Beijing Zoo received its breeding nucleus of three young pandas. The first captive birth occurred there in 1963. The baby of Li Li and Pi Pi was called Ming Ming. Li Li gave birth again the following year to an infant named Lin Lin. Both these births and all subsequent ones until 1978 were conceived naturally.

The first successful birth by artificial insemination also occurred in the Beijing Zoo, in 1978, and initiated the Chinese preference for this method of reproduction. Forty female pandas were artificially inseminated between then and 1982, but only eleven conceived and seven cubs were raised. By 1988 almost fifty litters of pandas had been born in captivity in China but only twenty-eight babies have been raised. As twins are common the survival rate was therefore considerably less than 50 percent. Chengdu Zoo has achieved ten births from which six cubs were successfully raised and the Beijing Zoo has been most successful with twenty-two births and fifteen survivors. There are about ninety pandas currently living in captivity in China. Approximately sixty of these are in zoological gardens, with the largest populations in Beijing, Chengdu,

Opposite
Hsing Hsing, who has
lived in Washington
DC's National Zoo
since 1972, is the only
breeding male panda in
North America.

Chongking, and Fuzhou. The remainder are in the forest reserve breeding stations. Wolong is one of these and has ten specimens.

But from all these animals an average of only three cubs are raised annually. If China had an exemplary captive panda breeding record there would be no complaints. However, the poor results have initiated much concern. In fact, virtually every aspect of China's management of captive pandas has been attacked.

The main criticism of China's breeding activities is that there is no program, and no nationally coordinated studbook. Contributing to the *International Studbook for the Giant Panda* would quell some of the criticism, for most of the pages referring to Chinese zoos in that publication are blank. Knowledge in the West of where China's pandas are may also generate more criticism of its efforts, but it would also prove that its zoos are at least exchanging information, which is the first component of any animal management plan. Also, apart from the four or five major zoo collections in China, numerous single pandas are kept in widely scattered zoos and apparently there has been little cooperation in the way of exchanges or loans, which happens frequently in Western zoos with other species.

Another major objection to China's conservation efforts is its desire to keep so many pandas in captivity, especially in the absence of a national management plan. Some of the $30 million spent to date on panda conservation has been used to build rescue stations and panda breeding centres. Facilities are still being built and pandas are still being captured despite the lack of breeding success in those facilities currently in use. An example is the Wolong Reserve's Research and Conservation Centre, built as a cooperative effort by the Ministry of Forestry and the World Wildlife Fund, which contributed $1 million. The Centre's captive breeding unit has outdoor facilities where potential mates can socialize, an important consideration for breeding pandas naturally. Yet only one panda has been born there since its completion in 1983, and the Centre is already very run down.

In China emphasis was placed on artificial breeding because it was believed to be the answer to the panda's incompatibility. When other zoo species are antagonistic to their partners the problem is usually solved by finding a new mate. The opportunity to do this has seldom existed for pandas outside China so the benefits of artificial insemination are obvious. But its use in China has been criticized because it is the approved method of breeding in the major zoos there which have a large number of captive pandas and therefore could breed naturally.

Having sufficient pandas and the opportunity to breed them naturally certainly exists in the zoos of Beijing, Chengdu, and Chongking, and in facilities like Wolong's Hetauping Breeding Centre, even though there is a surprising shortage of breeding males in China's captive panda population. Critics of China's concentration on artificial insemination tend to forget, or perhaps do not know, that in zoo circles sperm freezing, artificial insemination, and the developing practice of embryo transfer have all been touted as the most potentially valuable tools available for breeding endangered species.

Artificial breeding of pandas has been attempted in the West too. Madrid Zoo's Shao Shao gave birth after being successfully inseminated with sperm from London Zoo's Chia Chia, and one of her two cubs survived. Huan Huan at Tokyo Zoo also successfully conceived artificially and two of her three cubs survived. In 1983 after years of non-reproduction, the National Zoo's Ling Ling was also artificially bred by Chia Chia. As if aware that he must finally prove himself, her partner Hsing Hsing mated her the day before the insemination was to take place. To improve the chances of fertilization Chia Chia's sperm was also used as planned. The double mating was a success, but the first panda cub born in North America survived only a few hours. Using techniques that have decided human paternity cases, Hsing Hsing was declared the baby's father. He mated Ling Ling again successfully the following year without any prompting from the distant Chia Chia, but the resultant baby was stillborn. Ling Ling produced two cubs again in 1987 but both died.

The only facility in the West to have achieved repeated success in producing baby pandas and raising most of them is Mexico City's Chapultepec Zoo. Its pandas Pe Pe and Ying Ying arrived in September 1975 when they were both believed to be just one year old. Zoo officials refused to artificially inseminate Ying Ying, and for once there was no need as seven births resulted from natural conception and four of the cubs survived. They attribute their breeding success to three factors. The lack of disturbance and sedation as a result of not breeding her

Ying Ying, seen at right
with her last baby
Shuan Shuan at Mexico
City's Chapultepec Zoo,
is the most prolific
female panda in the
West.

The major problem in
breeding pandas is their
unsociable nature. This
pair (below right) on loan
to the Calgary Zoo in 1988
were more sociable than
most.

Tohui, (below),
born at the Mexico City
Zoo in 1981, will soon
be introduced to Chia
Chia, sent on loan from
the London Zoo.

artificially; their altitude, which at twenty-two hundred and seventy-five meters is similar to the pandas' natural home in Sichuan; and their diet which includes chicken, spinach, sugar, carrots, and milk. Yet these are supplements that all captive pandas receive. While husbandry and possibly altitude may play an important part in Chapultepec's success, it is the zoo's good fortune to have a compatible and fertile pair of pandas. This is highly unusual and is more than can be said for practically all other Western zoos that have pandas. Tokyo's Ueno Zoo is the next most successful panda breeding facility outside China. Its female Huan Huan has produced three cubs and two of these have survived.

Incompatibility is the reason why Madrid, Tokyo, and Washington resorted to artificial breeding in the first place. The fact that the only permanent pairs in North America and England, until 1985 when London's Ching Ching died, have not successfully produced and raised cubs indicates that there is more than technology or diet involved. Besides, both Washington and London have access to the finest zoo technological resources in the world. It cannot be altitude either, otherwise Beijing, which is little above sea level, would not have achieved such success. If the captive panda-raising record in China is mediocre, outside China it has been abysmal, apart from the success of Mexico City and to a lesser extent the Tokyo and Madrid zoos. There are three reasons for this. Compatibility has always been a problem; availability has been a major obstacle throughout their captive history; and initially they were difficult to sex.

The panda's sex organs are not visible externally. Only during the act of mating or if the animal has been sedated can its sex be accurately determined. The first pandas in the West were just too few and far between for any breeding activity to take place, and only recently have tranquilizing drugs improved to the stage where the sedation of rare animals is commonplace and without high risk. Consequently, many of the West's first pandas were wrongly sexed. Su-lin, Mei Mei, Sung, and Lien Ho were all thought to be females but when autopsied proved to be males. Chi Chi was also at first thought to be a female, then a male, then when in the zoo hospital for treatment was declared definitely a female. Inability to correctly sex animals is the breeders' second most serious problem. Coupled with poor availability the chances of breeding the first pandas were reduced to sheer luck. For years luck was absent from panda husbandry and probably still is.

When a mate of specific sex was needed during the early days of panda-keeping it was not often that trappers and native hunters could oblige. They tried, but when Western zoologists could not sex their own animals correctly they should not have expected that trappers would be more successful even though in most cases they seemed to believe what the suppliers told them. Pandas were so scarce anyway that it was a case of shipping the first one caught. Later on, when they became available to the West again, it was a case of "we will send you a nice pair of pandas, Mr. Prime Minister." It was an admirable gift. Whether the pandas would be compatible or would accept each other's attentions at the right time was unknown and probably did not seem significant at the time.

Detente and acquiring pandas were the important things.

When safer drugs to sedate wild animals were developed, sexing pandas became easier and opened up new horizons in their husbandry. But by then they were no longer available to the West. Before the breakthrough only London Zoo and Moscow Zoo had pandas outside China and they were forced to extreme lengths in their attempts to breed them. Moscow Zoo had a male called An An and the London Zoo owned the more widely known female, Chi Chi. She came into heat in the spring and fall, each time for between one and two weeks. After several years of sexual inactivity because a male was not available, "her system went into revolt" according to Desmond Morris, the zoo's Curator of Mammals, "when no mate responded to her calls and scent marking." By 1963 her heat periods "were intense and more prolonged," and as she ate very little during this time, being in heat for so long seriously affected her condition. She was even placed on a course of tranquilizers to calm her.

In February 1966 Dr. Morris went to Moscow to discuss the possibility of Chi Chi being introduced to An An. She was shipped to Moscow the following month. This was before the Convention in International Trade in Endangered Species came into effect and international shipments could be made far more quickly than they are today. Chi Chi and An An were immediately aggressive to each other and were quickly separated. A

FIGURE 5.

Pandas Born in Western Zoos

NAME	SEX	ZOO	DATE OF BIRTH	DATE OF DEATH
Sheng Li	F	Mexico City	10 Aug. 80	18 Aug. 80
Tohui	F	Mexico City	21 Jul. 81	
Chu Lin	M	Madrid	4 Sep. 82	
No Name	F	Madrid	4 Sep. 82	7 Sep. 82
Liang Liang	M	Mexico City	22 Jun. 83	
No Name	M	Washington	21 Jul. 83	21 Jul. 83
No Name	M	Washington	5 Aug. 84	5 Aug. 84
Xiu Hua	?	Mexico City	25 Jun. 85	
No Name	M	Mexico City	25 Jun. 85	27 Jun. 85
Chu Chu	M	Tokyo	27 Jun. 85	29 Jun. 85
Tong Tong	?	Tokyo	1 Jun. 86	
Ping Ping	M	Mexico City	15 Jun. 87	18 Jun. 87
Shuan Shuan	?	Mexico City	15 Jun. 87	
No Name	F	Washington	23 Jun. 87	26 Jun. 87
No Name	M	Washington	23 Jun. 87	23 Jun. 87
No Name	?	Tokyo	23 Jun. 88	

second attempt was made later in London, when Chi Chi and An An spent four weeks together. Although hardly together! For most of the time they were in adjoining cages because of their incompatibility. A mating was never achieved. Both animals died in 1972, having contributed much to the knowledge of panda behavior — especially social attitudes, temperament, and compatibility — but no baby pandas.

Poor availability was not the only problem Western zoos had to overcome. The seemingly cuddly panda's temperament and attitude to a potential partner, suspected in view of its solitary habits, were proved by Chi Chi and An An. Where its prospective mate was concerned the panda was not such a lovable creature, at least not in the zoo. In Western zoos and for Western zoologists there would be no more pandas for years and no opportunity to solve the incompatibility problem. They could only consider the enigma that was the panda, and continue to debate its origin.

Pandas are solitary animals in the wild, and although they are aware of others in the neighboring and overlapping territories from the scent marks they have left, they cohabit only during the short mating season. In captivity they have proved to be mainly monestrous, coming into season or estrus between March and May. Their behavior changes considerably at this time. They eat less and sometimes go off their food completely. They are more active, even agitated, and pace backwards and forwards making plaintive bleating sounds. The females increase their scent marking.

Unlike some solitary carnivores such as the tiger, leopard, or brown bear that can be housed with a mate all year in the zoo, a compatible pair of pandas is very unusual. Even if they do not live together all their lives, it is important that they at least tolerate each other during the short estrous period. Introductions have been difficult to achieve in zoos because courting and mating take place very quickly, usually in less than one hour after which they may take violent exception to each other. For the higher mammals synchronization of the reproductive cycles of both sexes must occur for breeding to take place, and why so few male and female pandas come into heat at the same time remains one of the unknowns of panda husbandry. Another is why the male should so frequently and so aggressively rebuff a female's overtures. Could this be connected with the lack of natural selection? In their area of study in the Wolong Reserve where seven adult males, six adult females, and several juveniles of varying ages lived, George Schaller and Hu Jinchu determined that "the largest and most dominant animals in the area do all the breeding. " This is usually the case with wild animals who participate in contests to maintain vigor. But it is seldom possible in the zoo environment where alternatives are unavailable.

In addition to removing pandas from the wild for their own safety there is another good reason to concentrate on conservation in the zoo. There is actually greater potential in captivity than in the wild for the production of baby pandas, if only this could be taken advantage of. Wild pandas rarely raise more than one cub and nothing can be done about it. In captivity no panda has attempted to raise more than one baby, even though in China twins are more common than single births and on one occasion a female at Shanghai Zoo gave birth to triplets. In contrast, of the twelve captive births outside China only four were twins. The others were singletons. This helped their chances of survival. If the success rate of raising panda cubs could be improved, almost double the wild population growth rate could be achieved in captivity.

Another advantage of zoos is that if a panda loses its baby within a few months of birth, or if it is necessary to remove it for hand raising, she will mate again during the next estrous period instead of waiting until the following year as the wild pandas are believed to do. Beijing and Chengdu zoos have taken advantage of this habit. After removing babies in March the females have been mated again soon afterwards and then given birth in September. Hand-raising baby pandas is difficult but is certainly not impossible. Su-lin, the very first panda to go West, was hand-raised, although she was probably one month old when she was abducted. The male Hsing Hsing that was sent to Washington Zoo in 1972 was about the same age when he was separated from his mother in the wild. The Shanghai and Beijing zoos have both successfully hand-raised baby pandas from birth. But it is a rare occurrence and has not been achieved in zoos outside China.

Another advantage of zoo breeding stems from the panda's increased longevity and breeding potential there, compared to the wild. Although the panda's life span in the wild will remain unknown for many more years until individuals can be tracked from birth to death, in captivity they can live for thirty years. This is a similar life span to the bears. A female panda that died at the Beijing Zoo aged thirty now holds the longevity record, and this is probably not exceptional since another female at the Shanghai Zoo lived to be twenty-nine years old. This life span is probably greater than they could achieve in the wild where the risk of predation increases with age. If the panda is capable of breeding almost to the end of its life span, as the bears are, there is obviously greater potential in captivity. A female at the Tienjin Zoo was still ovulating when she was seventeen years old and Washington's Ling Ling gave birth in 1987 at the age of seventeen years. Both pandas and bears are sexually mature when five years old. Therefore, in theory at least, a captive panda with a fifteen year breeding life span could produce an average of one and a half cubs annually or a total of three times more than a wild panda raising just one cub every other year.

To be of any value to the panda's survival prospects it is quite obvious that the captive breeding record must be improved in order to produce a net gain at the end of each year. Unfortunately in the West only the zoos in Mexico City, Tokyo, and Washington can contribute to this end because they currently have the only mature, breeding females outside China. Fifteen years after the West began to receive its lastest batch of permanent pandas, the number in captivity remains about the same. Sixteen were received, six have died, and seven have been born. Their sex ratio is eight males, five females, and four unsexed babies. But the situation is not as good as these figures make it appear, for when the sixteen animals were received they included seven potential breeding females. Now there are only four, although these are at least proven. The advanced technology and experience that these zoos contribute in solving panda reproduction problems will be invaluable even if the actual number of babies produced is not great.

If captive conservation is to be successful there are many puzzles that researchers must solve. There are the problems associated with incompatibility and the synchronization of breeding cycles. The relationship between diet and reproduction also deserves more investigation, and it must be determined if day length, temperature, or humidity affect panda reproduction. Artificial breeding procedures must be refined and improved and a sperm bank established. Above all, the captive raising record by both parent and foster parent must be improved because it is the major reason for the lack of reproductive success in captivity. Finally, there is a definite need to record all captive pandas in a studbook and a comprehensive plan must be developed for their management. If these breeding problems are not solved the confinement of pandas cannot be justified.

Zoo conservation is not a natural way to save animals. Only as a last resort should it be the only way. It is now generally accepted that a combination of both zoo and wild conservation is best for the panda, and there is certainly no shortage of advice and opinions on what should be done. The World Wildlife Fund, the International Union for the Conservation of Nature and Natural Resources, and the American Association of Zoological Parks and Aquariums have issued statements and guidelines. In 1986 the draft of a master plan to save the panda was produced by the World Wildlife Fund and the Peoples Republic of China. At its September 1987 meeting in Bristol, England, the combined position paper of the Captive Breeding Specialist Group of the International Union for the Conservation of Nature and Natural Resources and the International Union of Directors of Zoological Gardens, the world's most senior group of zoo administrators, supported this draft and emphasized, naturally, the captive breeding aspects. These included an international effort to promote captive breeding with a coordinated program that would not be detrimental to the wild pandas; an exchange of information and knowledge between Eastern and Western zoos; an international breeding program and long-term breeding loans and the inclusion of all pandas in the studbook; and the improvement of captive panda research and management.

Grandiose talk again? No, not any more. Already an unprecedented three-way international agreement has resulted in London Zoo sending Chia Chia on long-term loan to the Mexico City Zoo as a mate for Tohui who was born there in 1981. Chia Chia's journey took him via the Cincinnati Zoo, where the money raised during his three-month stay was donated to Mexico to help build the enlarged panda facility at Chapultepec Zoo. London Zoo is now panda-less for only the second time in thirty years.

Despite the poor breeding record there is a degree of security for pandas in captivity that does not exist in the wild where their numbers and chances of survival continue to plummet. Survival is the most important and most immediate concern, but freedom should be the ultimate objective. Only the preservation of the pandas' wild places and the pandas' eventual return there when it is safe to do so, can ever justify keeping them in captivity. When that time comes the only captive pandas should be those that are unquestionably non-breeders and need not be returned. In the meantime wild conservation must receive the same serious consideration and attention must be given to preserving not only the few remaining pandas but their remarkable mountains.

FIGURE 6. **The Distribution of Pandas in China**

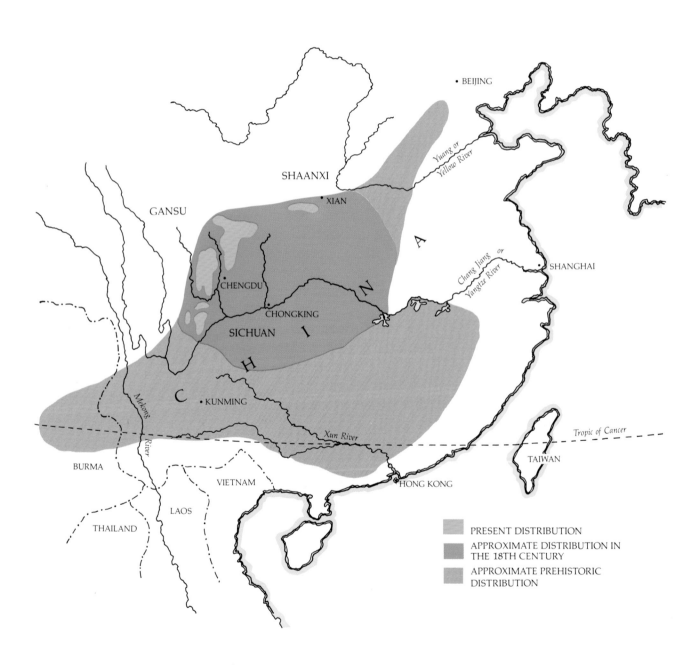

Conservation in the Wild

9

The unearthing of their fossilized bones all over China proves that pandas once lived throughout the country from the Tibetan plateaus in the west to the Pacific coastlands, north almost to Beijing, and south to the Vietnam border. Now their range is a fraction of that vast area. As the pandas' distribution declined so did their numbers. There were two reasons for this reduction in area and population. The first was a natural occurrence that happened long ago. The other was quite recent and can be blamed on mankind.

During the Pleistocene period, and especially towards its end, the earth experienced major environmental changes. It was the time that has become known as the Ice Age. World temperature fluctuations caused the great ice caps covering half of North America and much of northern Europe and Asia to advance and recede, and this produced extreme conditions in China. Alternating over many thousands of years between times when it was hot and moist and then cold and dry, the climatic changes affected bamboo distribution and growth and with it the panda's way of life. The result was extensive translocation and shrinking of its distribution in China. Then, in the years since the last retreat of the ice beginning about ten thousand years ago, the panda's continued decrease can be blamed on the rapid expansion of western China's human population which pushed the bear back into the remotest mountains.

One of the most dramatic reductions in the panda's range occurred in the relatively few years since Pere David visited western China in 1869. There are references to pandas living in Hupeh province on both sides of the Yangtze River at that time. This is six hundred and forty-four kilometers east of their present range in Sichuan and four hundred and two kilometers southeast of their isolated pocket of territory in southern Shaanxi. Arthur Sowerby who is considered to be an authority on China's wildlife in the 1930s believed pandas still lived close to Sichuan's border with Yunnan, just a few kilometers north of the Tropic of Cancer. Whether this was true or not the panda certainly had a larger range fifty years ago than it does today. It no longer lives in some of the areas where William Sheldon and Dean Sage shot their panda and followed the trails of others in the mid 1930s. Today, pandas are believed to survive only in several small areas of China's southwestern mountains, west of the metropolis of Chengdu and the teeming Sichuan plain and northwards to the ancient city of Xian. However, their secretive nature and the dense bamboo groves on steep mountain slopes have always made them difficult

Poachers are one of the most serious threats to the panda's existence in the wild.

Pandas have a home range of a few square kilometers which they mark with glandular secretions and they must check them periodically by sniffing.

to locate, and less than fifty years ago expeditions searched unsuccessfully for them in the mountains adjoining Chengdu. Even now, when researchers know that pandas live in their study area, they seldom see them for days at a time. Could they still survive elsewhere in the vast complex of forested mountains that reach west to Tibet and south to Vietnam? There has been little zoological exploration of those remote areas and there is evidence that the panda may have lived far west of its suspected present range, even to the edge of the Tibetan plateaus as little as fifty years ago. However, this has been disputed by some biologists.

Pen Hung Shou, a member of a Chinese Natural Resources Exploration Team, reported seeing a mother panda and her two cubs on the Tibetan plateaus in the summer of 1940, almost three hundred and twenty-two kilometers northwest of the species' previous range limit in southern Gansu. His report was doubted because pandas in the wild rarely raise two cubs and the open wind-swept plateaus devoid of bamboo were certainly not panda habitat. Yet in fairness to Pen, he did point out that the plateaus would be too bleak for pandas in winter and he suggested that as the pandas were still close to the mountains perhaps they migrated between them and the high open plains in summer. But with a plentiful supply of its favorite food on the mountainsides why would a panda migrate to the plains in summer, especially when the kinds of food available there also grew above the tree line a few thousand meters above its own bamboo zone. Even if Pen's observations were accurate and his theories plausible, those western pandas may not have survived to the present day.

The rapid decline of the panda's range is certainly one of the main reasons for its serious reduction in numbers. But other problems also affect the panda. Before conservation in the wild can be achieved these must be investigated, their causes identified, and solutions found. Only scientific study and research, not guesswork or philosophy, will conserve pandas in the wild. To begin these studies China has received aid from a number of sources and has itself poured money into panda conservation projects. Since the bamboo die-off and the plight of the starving pandas has drawn worldwide public attention, aid has been received in the form of funds, equipment, and scientific help and advice. The China Wildlife Association coordinated the drive for funds and the world responded, especially the children. A "Pennies for Pandas" campaign was organized in the United States and students in China held panda-donation days. The Japanese government donated almost a quarter of a million dollars and World Wildlife Fund Japan supplied twenty trucks for the panda rescue teams.

Intensive panda research began in 1980 when the World Wildlife Fund collaborated with China's Ministry of Forestry, the Ministry of Urban and Rural Construction and Environmental Protection, and the Academia Sinica. The World Wildlife Fund has since contributed over $4 million to research programs and facilities. The agreement between the World Wildlife Fund and China ended in 1985, but it has since been agreed that a long-term management plan will be developed for the panda and its habitat and that training will be provided for Chinese scientists.

Opposite Habitat
destruction, shown here
even in the Wolong
Nature Reserve, is the
main threat to the
panda's survival.

The Chinese government has itself spent almost $30 million on panda conservation. Some of this money has funded scientific studies but the bulk has been used to move peasants from areas important to the pandas' survival, to organize the rescue of starving pandas, and to build rehabilitation centres and breeding stations. In the wild, as in captivity, it is unlikely that the panda can be saved without a comprehensive management plan for its conservation. Such a plan cannot be produced and the necessary decisions made unless certain vital information is available. Many aspects of the animal's natural history must therefore be investigated. The panda's population dynamics, food preferences, predators, reproduction, and the relationship between mother and cub, as well as the human factors affecting its survival all require detailed study. Its activity periods, daily movements, and longer migrations in search of food all need investigation and evaluation. Field zoologists, reproductive physiologists, botanists, radiotelemetry experts who radio-collar pandas to track their movements, and biochemists who analyze the nutritional value of bamboo stems and leaves in the different seasons have already been involved in these studies and research.

In 1986 the World Wildlife Fund collaborated with China's Ministry of Forestry in drafting a master plan for saving the giant panda and its habitat. It recommended a modification of forestry practices and restoration of panda habitat to help perpetuate a viable population of free-living pandas. The improvement of captive reproduction to the point where zoo-born pandas could be released in the wild was also considered an important objective as was research into the panda's natural history and its application to the management of wild and captive pandas.

One of the first requirements of any wild animal management plan, in addition to money, is to determine just how many individuals survive in the wild. The first panda population census was conducted in the mid 1970s when three hundred participants estimated that about twelve hundred pandas had survived the first bamboo crisis. About 60 percent of these were in the reserves. It is thought that the continued decline since then, mainly as a result of poaching and another bamboo crisis, has reduced the wild population to between eight hundred and nine hundred pandas. Another census is now underway. From experiences with other species of endangered wild animals it is quite likely that the world will soon be informed that there are less wild pandas than anyone suspected.

Censuses also have the valuable additional benefit of determining exactly where the surviving animals are located. This permits their problems to be investigated and solutions offered. But, as in captivity, numbers are not always enough, and sometimes they bear little relationship to the species' survival prospects. In the panda's case there are major difficulties that could hamper its survival even if it received complete protection from poachers and no further loss of habitat. The most serious of these is the fragmentation of its small population. Within its reduced range the panda survives only in six separated zones spread over about thirty thousand kilometers of western China. Four of these tracts are totally within Sichuan province. Another, the largest, extends over Sichuan's border into Gansu province. The sixth is in Shaanxi province southeast of Xian, almost two hundred and forty kilometers north of the others.

Within these six areas there are about six thousand square kilometers of good panda habitat, and it is there that twelve reserves were established between 1963 and 1983 following the decree of the Third National Congress in 1959. Ten reserves are in Sichuan, one is in Shaanxi, the other in Gansu. Six hundred of the surviving wild pandas live in these reserves, but over half the total population live in Wolong, Foping, and Tangjiahe. The others have just a few animals each. To make matters worse there are no links of suitable habitat between the less populated reserves so there is no integration of their small and isolated populations.

The largest protected area for wild pandas is Wolong Nature Reserve, now a World Biosphere Reserve and just a few hours drive up rough mountain roads from one of the world's most densely populated regions. Established in 1975, Wolong covers two thousand square kilometers of Sichuan's Qionglai Mountains, adjoining the Chengdu-Chongking Plain where one hundred million people live — five million in the provincial capital of Chengdu. Seven species of bamboo grow on its mountain slopes that range in elevation from thirteen hundred meters to over

Opposite
Despite fantastic
scenery, only 15 percent
of the Jiuzhaigou
Nature Reserve is
considered good panda
habitat.

sixty-five hundred meters above sea level. About one hundred and forty pandas are believed to live in Wolong making it the most populated of all the panda reserves, just ahead of Tangjiahe. The first panda study in Wolong was aimed at discovering the extent of the animals' actual home ranges. Collars containing radio transmitters with sensors that denoted whether the panda was active or resting were fitted to five wild pandas to determine their activity patterns. Their home ranges were determined to be slightly more than five square kilometers. But all the ranges of the studied animals overlapped, those of the males each overlapping the ranges of several females. Within their home ranges the females were found to spend most of their time in a core area of about forty hectares.

According to the *World Wildlife Fund Yearbook* for 1983/84, five of the twelve reserves were surveyed by George Schaller and his Chinese co-workers in 1983. The purpose was to determine the status of pandas in each reserve and evaluate conservation problems. They also wanted to locate another panda study area where a new research base could be established in an ecological setting different from that at Wolong. One of the most disturbing findings of these surveys was the fact that the bamboo forest is very sparse in several of the reserves. Only about 15 percent of the Jiuzhaigou Reserve for example was considered good panda habitat. In Wanglang Reserve where the pandas had earlier suffered severely from the umbrella bamboo die-off, only about 35 percent was considered suitable for pandas. Forest clearing and farming were encroaching up the slopes, forcing the pandas onto the higher ridges and mountain tops. Fortunately other reserves have a good variety of bamboo species for their pandas.

In the southern-most reserve of Dafengding, isolated from all the others in two separate districts in the Liang Mountains, there were many species of bamboo acceptable to the pandas and the bamboo was growing at the right altitudes for them. Three of these bamboos grew fresh shoots for two months annually starting in March and ending in September, and provided a regular source of new food for the pandas and alternatives in the event of a die-off. With such a varied supply of food it is a pity that Dafengding has less than fifty pandas in its four hundred and fifty square kilometers. But it is still heavily forested, with the otherwise rare Chinese dove tree plentiful in its valley bottoms. It obviously has great potential for the introduction of pandas from other regions.

Because the panda's future is so entwined with bamboo, studies are underway to discover which species they prefer and if there is any seasonal variation in their choice. An analysis is also being made of the relationship between age and food preference, even to the size of the bamboo sections they bite off. At its station in Wanglang Reserve the Forestry Institute of Sichuan is attempting to speed up the slow growth rate of the arrow bamboo from seed. It is also trying to extend the bamboo's blooming cycle and vary its flowering times. The results of these bamboo studies will help to create the corridors that are urgently needed to link the isolated areas where the pandas now live.

Since the retreat of the last ice cap about ten thousand years ago, conflict with people has been the major threat to the panda's survival.

With most wild animals this conflict takes two forms. The first concerns the animals' raids on crops or herds. This is easier to control because the farmer or herder can be compensated financially for losses. The second is more difficult to regulate. It involves man's raids on the animals' environment for the resources found there including for the animal itself, the timber or other vegetation, and the land to grow crops. From the animal's point of view this is by far the worst kind of conflict. The loss of habitat, especially, is usually irreversible.

With the clearance of the lower mountain slopes for farming in many regions and encroachment even onto the higher and steeper levels, farmers' crops are replacing bamboo. Pandas could certainly find a greater variety of more nutritious foods in the fields adjacent to their bamboo groves. But there is no evidence that they raid these crops of corn, beans, or potatoes, as do other pest animals throughout the world. Pandas just pass through them looking for another patch of bamboo, so there is no direct clash between them and the peasants for that reason. The only incidence of antagonism was reported fifty years ago by William Sheldon who said that peasants in the heart of the mountains accused pandas of raiding their beehives. The Lolo tribesmen who killed Lieutenant Brooke when he entered their territory in 1910 apparently had no compunction about killing honey-seeking pandas either. But in most cases it is man's demands, first for the panda's lands and then for the panda itself, that have resulted in its now precarious position.

Destruction of the panda's habitat for firewood as well as to create farmland is another serious threat to its survival. In addition to the loss of the watershed which will eventually affect the livelihood of millions of people in the lowlands, the reduction of habitat for whatever reason is responsible for the isolated clusters of pandas. This separation of the few survivors into solitary groups would be a problem for any species of wild animal. For a specialized feeder that cannot migrate to other areas when its food supply dies, it is catastrophic. This separation can also be serious from the breeding point of view. A receptive panda female living in such a vast area with so few other pandas nearby may be unable to find a mate during her period of heat. Even if she does, the continuation of genetically healthy populations cannot be achieved with so few animals.

The loss of genetic variability through inbreeding results in lowered fertility, reduced survival rate of the young, and loss of the flexibility needed to evolve, which is an on-going process however long it takes for noticeable changes to appear. Inbreeding would therefore eventually affect a panda's ability to cope with changes in the environment, especially a crisis such as the loss of its bamboo supply. It has been calculated that a minimum closed population of seventy-five adult females and fifteen adult males is required to keep the rate of inbreeding at 1 percent, the maximum acceptable rate in the wild to maintain even the short-term health of the population. Many more specimens would be required in order to preserve the pandas' health and prevent the loss of evolutionary flexibility over a much longer term. But of all the reserves only Wolong, Tangjiahe, and Foping have enough pandas to maintain such healthy and genetically variable populations. The other reserves have so few pandas, some as few as twenty, that the variability cannot be maintained and genetic deterioration has already begun.

In an effort to solve this problem expansion of the existing reserves has been recommended, and then the connection of several to form a much larger unit. One government plan under consideration recommends joining Baishuijiang, Tangjiahe, Jiuzhaigou, and Wanglang reserves into one large unit. Elsewhere the establishment of corridors of bamboo between the reserves would allow the occasional migration of pandas into other controlled areas. Within each block it would be possible to link some of the isolated islands of panda habitat through protection and replanting. But with the pandas' rapid decline and the slow growth rate of bamboo, it is doubtful if there is time to do this. Even worse, some of the blocks of panda habitat that contain reserves are too widely separated to be linked by corridors.

Direct human attack on the pandas is the second most serious threat to their survival. They have been protected by the government since 1939 and it is illegal to kill them. But as with all rare animals, protection and scarcity have increased their value and consequently the demand. Poachers now actively seek pandas because of the high prices their pelts fetch in Japan and Hong Kong. The World Wildlife Fund says that about one hundred and fifty panda skins have been recovered from poachers in recent years, despite the severe penalties. Since 1987 China's courts have been able to impose the death penalty for panda poaching, but have yet to do so. In the same year twenty-six poachers convicted of killing six pandas received prison terms ranging up to life. Yet the poaching continues and pandas are not even safe in the reserves because of the shortage of anti-poaching patrols there. The recent decline of pandas in Wolong Reserve where they were not affected by the latest bamboo crisis has been blamed on poachers. In addition to the international poaching, pandas are still caught in snares set for musk deer. This is a thriving business to recover the deers' abdominal glands which contain up to thirty grams of wax-like musk — more valuable than gold to the perfume industry.

While human predation is a major hazard for the wild pandas, predation by their natural enemies is not considered a serious threat to their survival. In any case it would serve no useful purpose to eliminate all the natural predators of the panda in order to help the species survive. This aspect of wildlife conservation is fortunately not in vogue, as it was some years ago in less enlightened times. Such measures would result in the escalation of the deer and wild boar populations and this would have a serious effect on the habitat and consequently upon the pandas. It is already well known that there must be some control of the prey animals, and in the absence of predators starvation and disease become the limiting factors when their numbers explode.

As if the problems of poaching and loss of habitat were not enough, pandas are still being captured despite the Chinese government's efforts to stop the practice. Peasants continue to rescue them even though the bamboo shortage crisis ended some years ago. And rescued pandas are often not returned to the wild because every one of China's one hundred and seventy zoos naturally wishes to have one.

Most authorities believe that the pandas still in the wild should stay there, providing they are better protected and better managed. Hu Jinchu, the leading Chinese panda expert, believes that in order to save the species from extinction it is necessary to stop capturing pandas for zoos. But while it is easy to say that only pandas under the threat of death should be rescued, it is too much to expect peasants to make such a subjective judgment. Having instilled in the peasants a sense of pride and involvement to get their help in saving the pandas, the authorities find it difficult to control them without losing their cooperation. Without it the wild panda's chances would be very slim indeed. In any case, no more pandas should be brought into captivity unless they are clearly under threat in the wild. If it is managed properly, the current captive population is sufficient to continue the necessary research into improving reproduction.

Since better protection of the panda in the wild is a first prerequisite of its continual survival, the capture of all pandas outside the reserves and their translocation to underpopulated reserves that still have sufficient supplies of bamboo must be organized quickly. Reserves within reserves where all human activities and interference would be prohibited are under consideration. In such places the pandas would receive total protection from poachers, if such a thing is possible, and there would be no squatters, no logging, and no agriculture. Logged-out areas would be re-forested and corridors and buffer zones created. The corridors would connect isolated panda areas, allowing pandas to move freely in search of mates or find an alternate source of food when a bamboo shortage occurred in their own range. The buffer zones would be established adjacent to the reserves, and logging, settlement, and agriculture would be banned within them as well. The preservation of the panda's habitat will not only provide a haven for its return if captive breeding is ever that successful, but will conserve the other animals and plants that live there. All the world's efforts must unite to save the pandas, otherwise there is little hope for them.

Transient Pandas

10

The supply of detente pandas ended in 1982, dashing the hopes of several Western zoos. But they did not have long to wait before the process re-started — with a difference. The next wave of panda exports were temporary visitors only, destined to return to their native land after a few months. Beginning in 1984 zoos that stood little chance of getting pandas permanently, if only because their nation's capital already had a pair, were able to acquire them for a few months in summer. This practice, dubbed "short-term loans" but known as "rent-a-panda" by its detractors, caused more controversy than any previous conservation issue involving a single animal. It divided the North American zoo community and to a lesser degree the international zoo communiity, and harmed the relationship between the United States, China, and the international animal conservation movement.

In the opinion of many conservationists, short-term loans contributed to the panda's plight of approaching extinction. As the loans increased the concern and criticism escalated, but this controversy could not be solved objectively as had the other problems that had embroiled the panda for over a century. Equally convincing arguments were put forward by those who were for and those against loaning pandas. The opponents finally achieved their aim and stopped the loans, at least to the United States, by applying an international convention that prohibits commercialization of endangered species.

But before that happened there were many transient pandas paying brief visits to a number of zoos. In the summer of 1984 Los Angeles was offered at short notice a pair of pandas to help celebrate the Games of the XXI Olympiad. They were housed in the Los Angeles Zoo in an enclosure built for them in just six weeks. After three months these pandas visited the San Francisco Zoo, also for three months, and a panda rental fee was paid for the first time since Heini Demmer toted Chi Chi around Europe in the 1950s.

In 1985, after trying for many years to get pandas, the Metro Toronto Zoo received two on loan for the summer. Then, over the next two years pandas were exhibited for short periods in the Dublin Zoo, New York Zoo, Tampa's Busch Gardens, and zoos in Belgium, the Netherlands, and Japan. In 1988 a pair arrived at the Calgary Zoo, initially to celebrate the XV Winter Olympic Games, then on loan for the spring and summer; and the Toledo Zoo also received a pair. The same year, as their official contribution to the bicentenary celebrations, the People's Republic of

China has discontinued short-term loans of pandas to the United States because of the controversy surrounding them.

Los Angeles Zoo
received the first short-
term loan of pandas to
celebrate the Games of
the XXI Olympiad.

China sent a pair of pandas to Australia, where they were exhibited in both the Sydney and Melbourne zoos for three months each. They were then allowed to visit New Zealand for three months, where they were exhibited in the Auckland Zoo. Winnipeg's Assiniboine Park Zoo will probably be the only zoo to receive pandas on loan in 1989.

With the exception of such zoos as Los Angeles, Sydney, Melbourne, and Dublin, whose pandas were supplied for official commemoration purposes, the others paid rental fees in the form of "donations for conservation." These ranged from $250,000 US to $600,000 US, the standard fee being $100,000 US per animal per month. In addition there was usually provision for a percentage of the souvenir sales to be returned to China, plus some of the net revenue over an agreed amount. Some loans also involved services or training opportunities. Both Dublin's and Calgary's did, and the proposed Winnipeg loan includes provision for academic study for a Chinese student. Such cooperative exchanges are not a product of the sophisticated eighties. The precedent was set fifty years ago when the New York zoo sent books and scientific instruments to Chengdu in return for the panda Pandora, and one of the conditions for the shipment of Lien Ho to the London Zoo in 1946 was a year's free stay and study for a Chinese zoologist.

The benefits of short-term loans of pandas to other countries are international goodwill, education, publicity for the panda, and money. Their order of importance depends on the point of view. China regards the loans as goodwill gestures. Its furry black and white ambassadors draw international attention to the plight of their kind and permits for their travels here have been issued on these grounds. Traveling pandas are certainly seen by a lot of people who would not otherwise get the opportunity, and the people are made aware of the panda's plight. The recipient zoo also benefits from the increased local interest in its activities — from increased society membership and support, sponsorships and improved zoo viability and justification, and especially conservation and education programs.

In all of these areas the visiting pandas have done a tremendous job and have been a great success. In less than four months at the Metro Toronto Zoo the pandas were responsible for an attendance increase of seven hundred and fifty thousand and San Diego's attendance rose by six hundred thousand. An extra four hundred and seventy-two thousand visitors entered the Los Angeles Zoo while the pandas were there and Toledo Zoo's summer attendance doubled. All those zoo visitors, plus the many who attended Calgary, New York, Sydney, and the other zoos that received pandas on loan were exposed to a variety of conservation and education programs. In addition, millions of people living within the areas served by those zoos could not avoid the publicity bombardment about the pandas and their threat of extinction.

There were financial benefits as well — to both China and the zoos involved. China received loan income or donations of almost $5 million from ten zoos over a four-year period, plus significant amounts from souvenir sales and profit sharing. Although it was agreed that this income would be used in China for panda conservation purposes, many

Opposite
The largest attendance
increase occurred at the
Metro Toronto Zoo
when 750,000 extra
visitors came to see the
pandas.

In 1987, San Diego
Zoo's attendance
increased significantly
when it received pandas
on loan (below).

Opposite
The visit of Gong
Gong, the circus panda,
in 1988 caused almost
as much controversy as
the short-term zoo
loans.

believe that not enough has been done with the money to improve the panda's situation. But it is unreasonable to expect that China should account for every dollar it receives from panda rental. Besides it is likely that the loans are permitted by China as gestures of goodwill rather than as fund-raising events. In any event it must be remembered that the host zoos themselves have benefited from quadrupled souvenir sales, from having new or renovated panda facilities that could be used afterwards for other animals, and from having a variety of facilities — from washrooms to coffee shops — upgraded for the pandas' visits.

If the financial aspects of the loans were insignificant compared to the value of the international face-to-face publicity the pandas generated, why should these loans have caused so much apprehension? There are several reasons. Certainly there is a risk to the pandas' health and survival when international shipping is involved. Stress, injury, and to a lesser extent disease, are ever-present when wild animals are moved. However, modern shipping methods make the risks slight, and the shipping experience and the strange new environment are not sufficiently traumatic to affect a bear for the rest of its life.

A far more serious concern which was voiced by the World Wildlife Fund involves the potential capture of more pandas to increase the loans in order to take advantage of this new source of funding. But would this actually occur? It's difficult to say. Four pandas were available for loan when the practice began in 1984. By 1988 the number had increased to eight, but the demands for panda loans had escalated beyond the capability of these. The Chinese Embassy in Washington alone had requests for pandas from thirty institutions. If these requests were met conservationists' concerns that pandas would be removed from potential breeding situations for panda loans seem justified.

Furthermore Western critics did not believe that China was taking enough care to exclude animals of breeding age from the loans, and China's insistence that the pandas not be bred while overseas only increased the suspicion. Western fears materialized when the female Yong Yong, on loan to the Bronx Zoo in 1987, came into heat and a year's potential reproduction was lost. How ironic that the New York Zoological Society, which has done more for wildlife conservation than any other zoo or zoo society and many conservation organizations also, should have been responsible for precipitating this latest and greatest panda controversy.

The conservation community reacted promptly. The International Union for the Conservation of Nature and Natural Resources was the first to respond, and its 17th General Assembly, which met in Costa Rica in February 1988, proposed that loans of pandas should be completely compatible with an international breeding program. But short-term loans can never be compatible with an international breeding program, only with a Chinese breeding program. With one or two exceptions only China is in a position to loan pandas and to indicate that they are not required in its breeding program. The same organization also called for an end to all loans that do not contribute to the conservation of the species. Yet in the opinion of China and the zoos that seek pandas the

loans do contribute to the pandas' conservation through publicity and fund-raising.

Following these proposals the United States branch of the World Wildlife Fund went a step farther and urged the government to place an immediate and indefinite ban on all panda imports into America because the loans were hampering panda conservation by reducing the number of animals available for breeding in China. The organization also believed that pandas were being continually captured to augment the captive population in China, which was not self-sustaining.

Yet in 1984 the World Wildlife Fund not only had not objected to short-term loans but had given regional approval. The organization benefited financially when the pandas visited Metro Toronto Zoo, and the sale of a panda painting and signed prints by Robert Bateman raised $365,000. However, the organization has now reversed its stand and it urges the Chinese and zoos outside China to cease all exhibition loans.

The world's largest professional zoo and zoo staff organization, the American Association of Zoological Parks and Aquariums, was another major force that had raised doubts about panda loans. The organization was concerned almost from the beginning about its members receiving pandas and set up a Giant Panda Task Force in 1987 to investigate the practice. It issued guidelines and recommended that panda permits not be issued. But they were, including one to Tampa's Busch Gardens.

The pandas received on short-term loan by San Diego Zoo were trained performers. There is no doubt that zoo visitors enjoyed watching these activities.

Later more panda loan guidelines were drawn up. The most important were that animals should not be taken from captive breeding programs or from the wild and that the funds raised should be used for specific conservation programs. The board of the American Association of Zoological Parks and Aquariums voted unanimously to bind its members to these guidelines, and then forbade them to participate in short-term loans under threat of expulsion. It also received assurance from the United States Fish and Wildlife Service that no more import permits would be issued for pandas pending discussions with the Chinese authorities to determine the effects of the loans on the pandas and the extent that donations were helping endangered species. The participants were now in place — the International Union for the Conservation of Nature and Natural Resources, which wanted more controls placed on the loans; the World Wildlife Fund, which was now opposed to the loans; and the American Association of Zoological Parks and Aquariums, which forbade its members from receiving pandas. They were all set on a collision course with the Toledo Zoo, which had been planning its panda loan for some time.

Although both the World Wildlife Fund and the International Union for the Conservation of Nature and Natural Resources can pass resolutions and lobby governments to cease and desist practices that may be harmful to wildlife, they have no power to enforce their philosophies. This lies with national governments and the Convention on International Trade in Endangered Species of Flora and Fauna that was signed in

Washington in 1973 and has since been ratified by about one hundred nations. It bans commercial trade in endangered species and controls trade in others that are at risk of becoming endangered. The Convention is concerned only with international trade and it has no authority over the movement of animals or plants within the countries in which they live or are kept. It is the most significant international treaty protecting wildlife but its articles are not law. Rather the articles are applied under national import and export regulations. In Canada the Convention is administered by the Canadian Wildlife Service and in the United States by the Fish and Wildlife Service.

The Convention's species are included in three appendices. The most endangered ones, including the panda, are listed in Appendix I. Permits for these are issued only when certain conditions are met. The most important consideration is the non-profit one, for trade is allowed only when the transaction is "not primarily for commercial purposes." For example, it is considered to be commercialism if zoos increase their admission charge when they exhibit pandas, unless the extra revenue is clearly going towards panda conservation.

On May 23, 1988, the Convention's Secretariat confirmed its support in principle for exhibition loans that would be beneficial in furthering the cause of conservation. It also recommended that loans be kept to a minimum and that China no longer permit any zoo to capture wild pandas. And since loaning breeding pandas could reduce the captive breeding potential, the Secretariat stipulated that loans of pandas should only involve animals too old, too young, or otherwise unsuitable for breeding. At this time Toledo Zoo officials were continuing their efforts to acquire a Convention panda-import permit for the summer of 1988, a loan that China had already approved. Just two weeks after assuring the American Association of Zoological Parks and Aquariums that it would issue no more permits, the Fish and Wildlife Service granted Toledo a permit.

A few days later the World Wildlife Fund US and the American Association of Zoological Parks and Aquariums filed suit against the United States Department of the Interior and its agency the Fish and Wildlife Service for issuing this permit and sought a restraining order to prevent the pandas from leaving China. With the great increase in panda loan requests the two organizations felt that court action was the only way to stop the Fish and Wildlife Service from issuing further permits. The Toledo Zoological Society and the Toledo Zoological Gardens then entered the suit as intervening co-defendants. But the petition for the temporary restraining order was denied by the court, the pandas arrived in Toledo, and the case for a formal injunction was heard early in June.

In contradiction to the general conservation philosophy and China's policy not to send breeding-age pandas overseas, the visiting Toledo pandas Le Le and Nan Nan were from the Wolong Reserve's Research and Breeding Centre which was built and operated with World Wildlife Fund support. At eight years old the animals were clearly of breeding age. World Wildlife Fund US also objected to the perceived commercial aspects of the transaction, claiming that the bulk of the Toledo Zoo

Opposite
Medical checkups were
easy to conduct on the
San Diego Zoo's trained
pandas.

income from the panda loan was to be used for local zoo improvement, with only 10 percent of the expected income of $3.3 million being returned to China.

On June 17, 1988, the Honorable Norma H. Johnson of the United States District Court issued a preliminary injunction limited solely to preventing the Toledo Zoo from collecting additional fees for viewing the pandas, which had been set at two dollars for adults and one dollar for children. The zoo was restricted to recovering its panda loan expenses from souvenir sales, donations, and the expected increase in zoo attendance at the regular price. The Toledo Zoo and Society promptly filed an amended complaint against the Association and the World Wildlife Fund, seeking damages of $5 million for loss of revenue and a further $5 million for defamation of character.

The summer of 1988 passed. The Toledo Zoo kept its pandas for over five months and although it could not charge extra, the normal summer attendance doubled and souvenir sales were much higher than projected. The visit was a great success and the Association's Board of Directors did not expel the zoo from membership because its application for a permit pre-dated their policy decision. The court action appeared to have failed, for it certainly did not achieve its prime objective of blocking the importation. But it did initiate the series of events, including export bans, that can only assist the pandas' survival chances. Switzerland was the first to ban panda loans to its zoos and the Japanese Zoo Association then also forbade its members to receive pandas.

In the Federal Register of June 24, 1988, the United States Fish and Wildlife Service announced a moratorium on all panda permit applications, pending the development of interim rules on importations. It then refused the Michigan Department of Natural Resources a permit to import two breeding-age pandas for the 1989 state fair, a loan which had already been approved by China. It was refused because the fee might be used to expand the Wolong Breeding Centre and encourage the removal of more pandas from the wild to stock it. The Atlanta Zoo, which had already built the exhibit for two non-breeding male pandas aged eleven and sixteen years from the Shanghai Zoo, was also denied an import permit.

In June 1988 the Chinese government released a policy statement on panda loans. Only animals bred artificially or captured prior to the bamboo die-off in 1983 would be exported in future. Foreign zoos were expected to contribute funds or technical assistance to the Chinese Association of Zoological Gardens for panda conservation. The policy also called for improved management of the panda population in China, with the matching of all specimens for artificial breeding. All panda activities, including loan approval, became the responsibility of the Chinese Ministry of Forestry that controlled the twelve reserves. This ended claims of poor cooperation between it and the Chinese Ministry of Urban and Rural Construction and Environmental Protection that controlled the zoos. Three months later China suspended all panda loans to the United States and banned exports of the snub-nosed golden monkey as well, which had already been loaned to several zoos and was the number two Chinese attraction after the panda.

All the American organizations and the Chinese are now reviewing the guidelines for panda exports and developing a management plan. The Toledo Zoo affair that prompted so much controversy, in the end did more good than harm. It precipitated action that can only be beneficial to the panda. However, the harm caused to Chinese-Western relations by the criticism and court action is another matter. Yet critics were usually quick to point out that only the Chinese government's methods of saving the pandas were doubted, not its dedication. As a result of the new thinking import permits were then denied for pandas whose export had already been approved by China and this was followed by a ban on imports into the United States.

Soon after the Toledo Zoo affair another opportunity to criticize the exploitation of pandas occurred, this time involving the circus pandas. There are two of them that the West is aware of. One is an old animal that performs with the Shanghai Circus and has apparently visited Japan. The other is Gong Gong, the only animal star of the Great Circus of China. It has performed twice outside China, once in Thailand and then in Canada during the fall and winter of 1988. In Canada it was committed to participate in one hundred shows in three months. It was the first time a panda had performed outside Asia.

The original resolution of the International Union for the Conservation of Nature and Natural Resources recommended that the use of pandas in circuses should cease if the proceeds from their activities did not promote captive breeding. Since the World Wildlife Fund did not consider this to be the case with Gong Gong's circus performance they

condemned it and urged China to halt the practice. The decision to allow Gong Gong to accompany the circus was apparently made at the highest level in China, so once again criticism of his Canadian visit censured the Chinese government as well as the circus organizers. Most of the public anti-circus sentiment, however, was directed at the Canadian Wildlife Service for issuing a Convention import permit for what was believed to be a commercial activity. Attacking the permit-issuing body has become the approach most likely to succeed since the Toledo Zoo incident. It is preferred to a stand based on the less tangible issues of cruelty, morality, and the loss of breeding potential.

Yet the Canadian Wildlife Service held itself blameless. It believed that Gong Gong's presence could not increase circus attendance since it had been a sellout on its previous Canadian tour without him. In addition there was no increase in ticket price, and $1 million was being donated to an approved conservation project in China.

The main issue of the circus participation, as with the short-term loans, appears to be whether the publicity and the money are really helping the panda's cause. Publicity and money are usually the two most desirable commodities. On the subject of publicity there is no doubt that the organizers and Gong Gong achieved their aim. The media coverage of the main event and the criticism and picketing certainly drew national attention to the pandas and their distressing situation.

On the basis that pandas are their own best ambassadors Gong Gong was perfect, and if he is going to perform at all he might just as well do it where the big money can be raised to help his kind. But will his efforts help other pandas? They certainly will if the money raised is used for the approved purpose, which is called the Panda Protection and Conservation Centre. Some means of ensuring that the money reaches its destination can surely be found.

The funds raised in Canada for Gong Gong's visit had to be stipulated for a conservation project. After a visit to China the Canadian circus organizers chose to collaborate with the China Wildlife Conservation Association to create a new centre in Wolong Reserve. To determine its potential value scientists working in the reserve that already existed were asked their opinions. They agreed that a centre sponsored by Gong Gong would help to educate the peasants in the area about panda conservation efforts. With displays, videos, cartoons, and even comic strips it would explain the panda's situation in a manner the peasants could understand and the publicity would encourage their assistance. With portable equipment the message could be taken to the remotest mountain villages. The centre would also train wildlife enforcement officers and recruit and train peasants to act as anti-poaching patrols.

With the threat of loss of breeding potential seemingly alleviated only two concerns remain — those of inhumanity and morality. Is it inhumane to expose a panda to the stress of circus routine and the awe of thousands? The answer is no, because it is not the routine or the bright lights or the awe that are the problems. Exposure on stage is unlikely to be stressful to such a resolute animal as the panda, and for a solitary captive animal the routine of an act can only help to relieve the monotony of captive life. Training is usually considered the cruelest aspect of a circus animal's life anyway. But there is no question of using inhumane training methods for pandas, for such methods could not be continued on an overseas tour under the watchful eyes of the critics. If harsh treatment were the norm and it was discontinued the act would quickly deteriorate. In the case of Gong Gong's performance, emphasis was placed on the kind of activities that a panda may occasionally undertake in the wild, such as turning somersaults and sliding down snowbanks. And certainly his traveling arrangements could not be faulted, for his huge semi-trailer was equipped with a large air-conditioned room for him, a kitchen for preparing his meals, and quarters for his keeper and veterinarian.

Is it immoral for an endangered species and especially a panda to perform and entertain people? Other endangered species do. Elephants perform in zoos, tigers and leopards in circuses, and killer whales in marine aquariums. Similar to Gong Gong their performances are based on an extension of their natural behavior. This may not condone the practice, but it certainly makes it more acceptable to the majority. People enjoy watching the animals, are perhaps educated by the process, and the exercise and activity keep the performing animals in better condition than their caged counterparts. The close bond that exists between the pandas and their keepers allows medical tests to be performed without sedating them and producing physiological changes that could be misleading and result in inaccurate test data.

The circus pandas are not the only performers. Basi and Yuan Yuan, which the San Diego Zoo received on loan from Fuzhou Zoo in 1987, both performed daily for the zoo's visitors. They provided a much better insight into panda behavior than would have been gained from watching them sleeping next to their bamboo pile. Such inactivity was the only real criticism of zoo visitors who had sometimes waited for hours to see the pandas in their local zoo.

But Gong Gong was just an interloper in the main panda event of the decade — the transient panda controversy. If performing pandas never appear again in the West, there is still a future for zoo loans. Eventually, when a management plan and studbook prove beyond doubt that certain pandas are definitely non-breeders, what better purpose can they serve. Short-term loans would be a valid use for the aged and the infertile, and even for fertile males whose genes were in cold storage. Loans could be of tremendous value to panda conservation if they were properly regulated, and the transients could serve as ambassadors at large to the benefit of their species without affecting any breeding plans. Hopefully, despite past criticism, China's government will permit this arrangement to continue.

In the meantime the ban on imports and the threat of expulsion facing members of the American Association of Zoological Parks and Aquariums if they participate in panda loans is academic anyway, at least for its American members. China has stopped all loans to the United States and now has the last word whatever the outcome of the current deliberations. The World Wildlife Fund has urged the Chinese and zoos outside China to cease their involvement in panda loans beyond 1988, and will not associate itself with any further transactions. So short-term loans certainly had a shorter term of life than anyone expected. They began in 1984 and will likely end, for the time being at least, in 1989, when non-breeding pandas Cheng Cheng and Rong Rong visit Winnipeg's Assiniboine Park Zoo. In return a donation will help to build the panda breeding centre operated by the Chengdu Zoo.

The Assiniboine Park Zoo, a medium-sized facility recognized as one of the nicer zoos in North America, has for years been quietly doing the things that nowadays are said to justify a zoo's existence. It has attracted and pleased an average of almost one million visitors annually over the last decade and has certainly aided conservation by producing many endangered animals. But with just a fraction of the budget of many similar-sized zoos the education and research aspects of zoo justification have been limited. Owned and operated by the City of Winnipeg and supported by the Zoological Society of Manitoba, the Assiniboine Park Zoo did not pursue pandas, as most zoos did through years of lobbying and visits to China. It merely accepted a gracious offer from the People's Republic of China to the people of Manitoba. Now, thrown into the international spotlight by the loan, it is cast by some as the latest villain in the panda's troubled times. Yet it is optimistic about the outcome of the panda visit and the ultimate conservation of one of the world's most unusual animals.

A Selected Bibliography

Allen, G. M. 1938. The Mammals of China and Mongolia. Vol. II, Part I. Amer. Mus. Nat. Hist.

Bertram, B. C. R. 1987. The Giant Panda Studbook 1987. Zoo. Soc. London, London.

Carter, T. D. 1937. The Giant Panda. Bull. New York Zool. Soc. 40, 6-14.

Crandall, Lee S. 1964. The Management of Wild Mammals in Captivity. Univ. Chicago Press, Chicago.

Davis, D. D. 1964. The Giant Panda. A morphological study of evolutionary mechanisms. Fieldiana: Zool. Mem. 3, 1-339.

Ewer, R. F. 1973. The Carnivores. Cornell Univ. Press, Ithaca. New York.

Farrell, A. (Editor). 1984. WWF Yearbook 1983/84. WWF. Gland, Switzerland.

Flower, W. H. and R. Lydekker. 1891. Mammals Living and Extinct. Black, London.

Graham, D. C. 1942. How the baby pandas were captured. Bull. New York Zool. Soc. 45, 19-23.

Harkness, R. 1938. The Lady and the Panda. Nicholson and Watson, London.

Heuvelmans, B. 1958. On the Track of Unknown Animals. Hart-Davis, London.

McKinnon, J. and Qui Minjang. 1986. Masterplan for saving the Giant Panda and its habitat — a preliminary discussion draft. WWF/PRC.

Morris, R. and D. Morris. 1966. Men and Pandas. McGraw Hill, New York.

O'Brien, S. J. 1985. The Ancestry of the Giant Panda. Nature Sept. 12-18, 102-107.

Pen, H. S. 1943. Some Notes on the Giant Panda. Bull. Mem. Inst. Biol. Peiping. 1, 64-70.

Phillips, C. (Editor) 1986. WWF Conservation Yearbook 1985/86. WWF. Gland, Switzerland.

Pocock, R. I. 1921. The external characters and classification of the Procyonidae. Proc. Zool. Soc. London. 389-442.

Roberts, T. J. 1977. The Mammals of Pakistan. Ernest Benn, London.

Roosevelt, K. 1930. The Search for the Giant Panda. J. Amer. Mus. Nat. Hist. 30, 3-16.

Roosevelt, T. and K. 1929. Trailing the Giant Panda. Scribner's, New York.

Schaller, G. B., Hu Jinchu, Pan Wenshi and Zhu Jing. 1985. The Giant Panda of Wolong. Univ. Chicago Press, Chicago.

Schaller, G. B. 1986. Secrets of the Wild Panda. Nat. Geo. Vol. 169, No. 3, 284-309.

Schmidt, J. 1988. The Long Road Back. Equinox 39. 32-47.

Sheldon, W. G. 1975. The Wilderness Home of the Giant Panda. Univ. of Mass. Press, Amherst.

Zhu Jing and Li Yangwen, (Editors). 1980. The Giant Panda. Science Press. Beijing.

Index